BERWYN ___IC LIB.
3 ' REET

VALGLING 824-

AU

AU DISCARD

D1068737

Glint

BERWYN PUBLIC LIBRARY
34th STREET

Glint

Joseph Valentinetti

DISCARD

St. Martin's Press
New York

GLINT. Copyright © 1995 by Joseph Valentinetti. All rights reserved.
Printed in the United States of America. No part of this book may be
used or reproduced in any manner whatsoever without written
permission except in the case of brief quotations embodied in critical
articles or reviews. For information, address St. Martin's Press, 175
Fifth Avenue, New York, N.Y. 10010.

LIBRARY OF CONGRESS CATALOGING–IN–PUBLICATION DATA

Valentinetti, Joseph.
    Glint/Joseph Valentinetti.
      p.   cm.
    "A Thomas Dunne Book."
    ISBN 0-312-13082-1
    I. Title.
    PS3572.A397G55   1995
    813'.54—dc20   95-1737
                                 CIP

First Edition: June 1995

10 9 8 7 6 5 4 3 2 1

For

Walter and Nettie,

Mary,

Paul and James

Glint

One

Quitman O'Neil sold cars. "I roll iron and rubber over the curb," he would say. He met both Helen and Maria in the same way: He sold a car to each of them.

When Quitman first saw Helen it was dusk. The car-lot lights hadn't come on yet. The low sun spilled her shadow a long way across the asphalt. When he approached he already had the keys to a certain car in his hand. He picked it out for her when he noticed her deliberate way of walking as she came onto the lot.

Instead of beginning with "Hello" he began with, "There's something right over here." He gestured with a slight wave and she followed him to the passenger side of a four-door. "Come a little closer. Watch this." She moved forward, looking around furtively, as though she were unsure of just what he was getting at. "Now watch," he said again as he slid the key into the lock. "See? The second you put the key in, the interior lights come on. Good for safety, don't you think?"

The car had sat locked up tight all day in the baking sun and now when he opened the door in the cool evening air the deep, rich aroma of the leather wafted in their faces.

Helen was relaxed, almost nonchalant, as she eased the Cadillac onto the street.

"If you don't mind my saying so, Helen—may I call you Helen?" Quitman began.

"Please do," she said, glancing over at him.

"Well, if you don't mind, Helen, I think this car suits you very well. I hope you like it."

She thought for a moment. "I wouldn't want to spend too much. Just how much do you think the payments would be?"

"I understand your concern. There are times when we all have to be cautious not to exceed our limits. Was there a figure you were thinking of?"

She stiffened, condescended a smile, "It's not a question of that. It's more a question of priorities." Except for the purring of the climate control they rode in silence until she asked, "Does the radio work?"

"Yes."

"I think anything more than five hundred a month would be ridiculous."

Quitman felt a warm glow come over him. There, bathed in the amber luster of the dashboard lights, he took a second to let the magic words wash over him. He felt them splash over his skin like that split-second feeling when your flesh adjusts to the bath water and you swell with contentment. Five hundred dollars was a very good opening bid, so he said, "If I could manage to get it for you for that would you consider buying tonight?"

*

Still more than half asleep, Helen stretched across the king-sized bed and dragged the other pillow close to her face. She lay for several moments inhaling his aroma in easy breaths. Though Quitman had offered, she rejected the lubricated latex of a condom for the pulse of the flesh itself. The halo of heat as it entered her touch. The tactility afterward.

2

She slid to the edge of the bed, got her robe, and maneuvered into it before letting the covers fall away. She walked to the window where the early morning sun streaked across her face, highlighting her long slender nose and the lines that radiated from the corners of her green eyes. In the driveway below the window, Quitman hosed the sudsy water from the broad hood of the Cadillac; the water rolled in sheets off the fenders and gleamed in the sun. When she had bought the Cadillac from him six months before, she wasn't sure what had prompted her to do it. For several weeks, she was surprised to see it in her driveway. Then Quitman had called and asked her to dinner. She had been both titillated and repulsed by the pseudo-incestuous implication of a lover twenty years her junior. A thrill had run through her when he touched her hand at the dinner table. She overcame the desire to swallow hard.

Quitman kicked off his wet shoes as he came back into the house, "Good morning. Always sleep so late?"

"Not usually." She felt him behind her; his hand slid around her waist.

"I couldn't resist hosing off your Caddy," he said.

"Looked more like a complete wash job to me," she replied, leaning her head back and nuzzling it against his shoulder.

"It was really just a touch up. I like that particular shade of Cadillac blue. They only used it for a short time. When it's clean it has tremendous depth, like you're staring into cold clear water."

"Blue's always been a particular favorite of mine."

The knobby terrycloth, warmed by the stove, comforted his chilled hands. "You can ignore the bacon for a second, huh?"

The nerves in her skin danced under his touch. "Ooh, your hands are cold," she said. She turned; to her

3

disappointment he kissed her lightly. "I'll be done here in a moment. Do you like French toast?"

He nodded; licked his lips.

"Go wander around or something. I'll call you when it's done."

He lifted a framed photograph from the bookshelf. It pictured a broad-jawed man as much senior to Helen as she was to Quitman. "Is this your husband," he called out, "in the photo?"

"It was. He passed away five years ago."

"I'm sorry," he said, as a flutter of emptiness brushed through him. He replaced the photograph and, absently trailing his finger along the edge of the shelf, moved further into the room. "What did he do?"

"He worked for the government. In Denver. We lived there till he passed away."

Quitman opened the drawer of the desk, "Why here from Denver?"

"My sister-in-law was here," Helen said as she came through the doorway, "but almost as soon as I got here, her husband got transferred and they moved."

"So much for family."

"So much for family. What about you?"

"No family to speak of. Parents are dead."

She felt an invisible shiver. As much from the matter-of-fact way he said it as from the fact itself. "I'm sorry."

He ran his fingers into his unruly hair and clasped his hands behind his head. "Thanks. So am I."

She felt more comfort in his tone now. More warmth. The sweet cinnamon aroma from the toast drifted into the room. "Can you smell that?" she asked. "It's almost ready. You wash up, I'll put it on the table. Coffee black?"

"Cream and sugar."

She turned back into the kitchen. Quitman looked

down and saw a silver dollar in a plastic cover on the front corner of the desk. He picked it up and stared at it through the plastic.

She called to him from the kitchen. He slipped the coin into his pocket. It wasn't the monetary value that intrigued him, if it had any value beyond a dollar. He had just never seen one with the year of his birth on it before. 1964. Lucky, he thought.

"This is good," he said, cramming a triangle of syrup-dripping French toast into his mouth. The shock of the sweetness made his jaw cringe.

"Thanks."

"So you moved here after Mr. Costello died?"

"Yes. But my husband's name wasn't Costello, it was Meyers, Jim Meyers." Quitman looked at her, puzzled. "We were married in the sixties. It was popular for women to keep their maiden names."

"Even then."

"Even then. Even when you were just a baby."

It suddenly seemed peculiar to him. Being in this woman's house, fresh from her bed, eating her cooking, and she was the age of his mother. He scrutinized her face. Would my mother be like this now, if she'd have lived? Wrinkles sprouting from the corners of her eyes and little pinch marks at the corners of her mouth? If only dad had died would she be fresh from screwing someone else, maybe even someone younger than me? A flush of disgust for Helen washed over him, Why are you doing this? he wanted to ask her, but said instead, "Not so much of a baby now."

She blushed slightly as she pulled a tiny nibble of food off her fork with her white teeth.

"Was that his desk?"

"Yes, why?"

"Just looks untouched."

5

"It is. Don't even know why I brought it with me. Sentimental, I guess."

"I like that," he said. He felt a warmth for her. "That's nice."

"I guess it is."

"I like lazy days like this," he said, reaching over, caressing her cheek. "I think Baby could use a nap."

Phantom icy fingers waltzed up her spine. She clasped his hand in hers, "Can I tuck you in?"

Two

Quitman's habit was to pick up two-dozen doughnuts on the way to work for himself and the other salesmen and managers on duty with him. His nimble Porsche serpentined into the parking space. As he shut the car door he could see Artie, the counterman, already preparing his order. His mouth salivated from the rich scent of caramelized sugar. He tucked in the tail of his shirt and looked casually around the small L-shaped shopping center. At the elbow of the L, a storefront he'd never noticed before caught his eye. A simple gold-leaf sign under a green and white striped awning read COINS.

He slid the flimsy box of two-dozen assorted onto the passenger seat. Though the coin shop was less than fifty yards away, he drove there. He pushed through the buzzer-released iron gate inside the front glass door and realized he was in a cage, surrounded with wrought iron worked into curlicues and spirals in an attempt to belie its purpose.

A scrawny, spectacled man looked up from the rear of the shop, his right eye exaggerated by the spectacle loupe in front of his lens. He inspected Quitman for long moments, then returned to his work without a word.

Quitman inched along the glass cases, inspecting the coins. Each coin had been carefully encased in a sealed plastic bag and stapled to a descriptive card. One display case was marked COLONIALS and he stared for several minutes at the coin labeled PIECE OF EIGHT. A small placard under it read, "The most circulated and trusted coin of colonial America." "I'll be damned," he murmured.

"Interesting, isn't it?"

Quitman glanced up to find the scrawny man standing before him, the loupe now swung away from his lens. His less-than-white dress shirt hung from his shoulders as though still on a hanger rather than a body. His face hung, expressionless, in the air.

"Very."

"Are you a collector?" the precise voice asked.

"No. I . . . I don't know anything about it. Just a little curious."

"About anything in particular?"

"No. Well, yes. Got any coins from 1964? I realize that's not very old, but, like I said, I'm curious."

"Yes. Yes I do. Follow me," the eroded little man said.

He led Quitman down the aisles of glass cases to one in the rear. He reached inside and produced a square of blue felt that cushioned six brilliant coins.

"You may view them through this," he began, handing Quitman a lighted magnifier, "for a more satisfactory inspection." He took a step back and bowed his head, perhaps to be obsequious. He grinned slightly, apparently happy with his invisibility.

Quitman studied the coins haphazardly, not knowing what to look for. Except for being very shiny, they were much like every other coin he had ever seen.

Sensing his confusion, the little man unclasped his skeletal fingers and stepped forward. "Flip over the half-dollar, the fifty-cent piece there on the lower right, and look at the reverse, just below the olive sprig."

"You mean the tails side?" Quitman turned the coin face down.

The little man smirked, "Yes, the tails side."

"What about it?"

"Do you see the letter 'D' printed there?"

Quitman squinted through the magnifier. "What's it mean?"

"It simply means that it was minted at the Denver facility."

"Denver?"

"Yes. And the fact that it is noted on the reverse gives that coin some small margin of value."

"Really?"

"Not much, you understand. But 1964 to 1967 are the only fifty-cent pieces with the mint identification on the rear; so as I said, it gives them some small margin of value—among clad coinage, that is."

Quitman's head was beginning to muddle. The man's precision and jargon were confusing. He was telling Quitman more than he ever wanted to know. Impatiently he said, "Isn't there something missing?"

"Missing?" asked the crumbling man.

"Where's the silver dollar?"

The little man smirked in open disdain, "There isn't one."

"I have o—" Quitman stopped himself from admitting what he had in his pocket and paused to study the skeletal face before him. "I've seen one."

"Impossible. Where did you see it? No. That's impossible, completely impossible. There simply were none made."

"I saw it, what can I say?"

"Was someone, perhaps, trying to sell it to you? Someone was playing a joke, or worse, a trick. The last silver dollar minted in this country was in 1935. You must beware, my friend, to buy only from reputable dealers—unless, of course, you knew what you were doing. Forgive me if I say so, but you do not."

"I've seen newer silver dollars than 1935."

"A misnomer. They have been striking the one dollar coin again since 1971, but it is not a silver dollar."

"There's no possibility?"

"Of a 1964 silver dollar?" He slowly removed his eyeglasses and looked Quitman in the eye, "None."

The little man stood with his hands clasped behind his back, his head craned forward on his neck, and watched Quitman get into his car and squeal away from the shopping center. He turned and walked to the rear of his shop maintaining the same sulking posture, the same deliberate speed. He stood motionless for several minutes, looking at nothing except his inner thoughts. He then drew his right hand from behind his back and lifted the phone receiver.

*

Sitting at his desk, Quitman slid the coin from his pants pocket and laid it on the blotter to examine it for perhaps the thirtieth time since leaving the coin shop. He held it between his fingers and ran his nail along the ridged edge and he could hear a faint clicking like a playing card held in the spokes of a lazily spinning wheel. He looked up at Martinez, "Marty. How can you tell if a coin is real or not?"

Marty sat about ten feet away, his swivel chair at full tilt and his clasped hands rested on his developing belly. From his position he could see the car lot by simply turning his head but he didn't.

"You think I know?" He ran the flat of his palm along the side of his manicured hair.

"Just asking."

"I don't know."

"I gathered that," Quitman said, sliding the coin in and out of its plastic pocket.

Quitman had worked sales floors before and always made reasonable money but he never really sold a car, never really had fun at it, until he came to West's Classics and teamed with Marty. Marty didn't care about cars, he cared about selling. Working with people to help them get what they want; if he got what he wanted from it in the bargain, all the better. Marty didn't really sell anything but air. Dreams. He took his customers out and *"parked them under the oak tree in the sunset"* and let them sell themselves. Quitman had gone with him on a few demo rides at first. Marty would drive people to the circular drive in front of the Red Lion Hotel, get out, and tip the doorman to open the door for his guests. Back them up so they could take it in: their car, their doorman, their luxury hotel, their new life. Let them get behind the wheel, see what it's like to be rich. See what kind of respect you'd get if you only drove around in this kind of car all the time. Imagine that.

"What's got you? Your mood sucks," Quitman said.

"It's the rain. Fucking weather. Slow month. No money. I did a callback on a guy I been working with for weeks and the prick tells me he bought a car down the street. This is after I romanced the guy, put the smell of leather up his nose. You can't trust anybody." Marty waved a vague hand toward the window. "Want more?"

"No thanks." Quitman slid the coin back in his pocket.

"Can I use your demo tonight?"

"The Porsche?"

"How many demos you got?"

"The Porsche."

"The Porsche, then."

11

"Will it improve your mood?"

"I doubt it."

"What will?"

"Less questions."

"And the Porsche?"

"And the Porsche."

❧

The little man slouched down in the leather chair, almost consumed by it. Across the room Henry Lyman—a man who, if you sliced him right, you could have made four Emile Hacketts out of—poured Martell into a snifter as he spoke.

"This is a little cloak and dagger isn't it, Hackett? Not wanting to discuss whatever this is about on the phone. I hope it's worth it."

"I believe it is, Sir. We can't be too careful."

Henry Lyman crossed the room and deposited his bulk in an identical chair facing Hackett. The cushion hissed its resentment and the leather crackled. His face was free of worry, silver hair brushed out from his head and eyebrows. "What is it then?"

"I believe, Sir, that I can acquire a coin that would be the glory of your or any other collection. A coin so rare—"

"What coin, Hackett?"

"The 64 D silver dollar."

"Is that old rumor cropping up again? What is it, once every seven years that rumor surfaces, or is that locusts?" he asked rhetorically and without humor.

"This time I think there's some truth to it."

"You've seen it?"

"No."

"You know who has it?"

"No."

Lyman rose abruptly, his broad round shadow casting itself across Hackett. "Then what is this? Money? Is that what you want? Money? Money to go on some kind of a treasure hunt? Hackett, you're wasting your time and, more important, mine."

Sweat peaked through the pores on Hackett's brow. "If I may explain, Sir." Lyman remained standing, showing his back to the little man. Hackett saw the rolls of fatty flesh that gathered at the back of Lyman's collar. "A man came into my shop to inquire about it. He pretended to be browsing, but I believe that his inquiry was his specific purpose in coming. I feel certain he has seen it."

Lyman turned. The blandness was back in his puffed, hooded eyes. His hands engulfed the brandy glass. "What's his name?" he demanded.

"I don't know. I couldn't let him know I was interested, or even that I believed that such a thing existed, you understand."

"I do. Go on."

"He was looking first at a 'Piece of Eight' and I assumed that he was perhaps a novice and I could help guide his initial selection."

"Get top dollar in other words."

Hackett bristled at the crassness of Lyman's remark but went on, "When I spoke to him, his first question concerned coins from 1964. He was no collector, I'm sure of that. He even called the reverse the 'tails side.' " Hackett attempted a smile. His deeply yellowed teeth showed for a second then disappeared behind tense lips.

"That's all just fine. But if he does know where it is, or if he has it, or if he knows how to get it, how do you propose we find him? You don't even know his name."

"But I know his license-plate number." The little man smiled again. "It was a dealer's plate. He is a car salesman."

❦

"VanDyk."
"This is Henry Lyman calling."
"Yes, Sir."
"The coin dealer, Emile Hackett, he knows a license number that I'd like to know."
"Yes, Sir."

❦

Hackett paused his dusting in mid-swipe and looked up when the entry bell at his coin shop dinged. When he recognized Lester VanDyk his throat tightened. His duodenum vibrated nervously. A rush of adrenalin blurred his vision. Hackett had seen VanDyk only once before. They were both present at a coin purchase. VanDyk was there to protect the interests of Henry Lyman and when things began to go awry he did just that. Swiftly, silently, without a change of expression, without missing a beat. VanDyk's presence here was, at once, clear.

VanDyk stared at Hackett for long moments, then, reaching over the counter he turned the "Closed" sign to face the street. The iron accordion gate rasped as he yanked it shut across the front door.

Hackett, still standing, with his feather duster poised, shouted out, "What are you doing, Mr. VanDyk?" He laid down the duster, fighting back the trembling he heard in his own voice. "Please answer me, Mr. Van-Dyk. What are you doing?"

VanDyk's eyes were a lilting blue. His soft blond hair, cut businesslike, complimented the healthy gold tone of his skin. Even his voice rang with sincerity when he spoke. "I just need a moment of your time, Emile."

Tension swelled in Hackett's blood. He felt his pulse throb in the backs of his hands and at his throat. He backed up with small, cautious steps, hoping his retreat would go unnoticed. Drops of sweat spilled over his brows into his eyes, stinging with their salt. He let out a meaningless sound, an involuntary squeak. He spun and fled toward the back. VanDyk darted after him, hurdling a glass case gracefully, without even looking at it, his eyes never leaving his prey. Hackett fumbled at the door of his office with all ten of his thumbs. He stumbled through the doorway. He tripped, banging his head on the wooden arm of his desk chair. He flung the chair aside and scampered the few remaining feet to the desk. As he grabbed the handle of the bottom drawer VanDyk seized his arm.

"Not a gun, Emile. You weren't going for a gun, were you?"

The eyes of china blue were only inches from his own. VanDyk had his forearm in his viselike grasp. Hackett's fingers began to numb. He whimpered, "No, nothing like that."

Without letting go of the arm, VanDyk flung Hackett's skin-and-bones body to one side, leaned forward, and slid open the drawer. Even wrapped in the oilcloth the shape was unmistakably a gun. With his one hand already at the elbow he placed his other hand at Hackett's wrist and slammed the exposed part of the arm down on the edge of the desk. The cracking wasn't even as dramatic as the sound of a lobster claw in the jaws of a pliers, still, the arm dangled, broken. Hackett clutched it as he crumpled to the floor.

"Just a moment of your time, Emile."

15

*

VanDyk stationed himself across the street and down the block from the main driveway to West's Classic Auto Sales. The digital clock on the dash said 2:30. He'd been waiting seven hours. Alternately he drank tepid coffee from a pump thermos on the seat beside him and urinated into a cardboard milk carton that sat on the floorboard.

"He's not dead," he said into the car phone, "just wishes he was. I'm waiting for the guy now. I've got to sight him before I go in."

"Keep me informed," Lyman said, hanging up.

VanDyk spied the Porsche as it crawled into the driveway and up to the building. He checked the license plate and then the driver through field glasses.

*

"Thanks for the use of the car, O'Neil."

"The Porsche?"

Marty sniggered. "The Porsche."

"No problem, Marty," Quitman answered. "Improve your mood?"

"What do you think?" Marty said, ducking into his cubicle.

It was early afternoon. The sun sat high and hot in the sky, its edges blurred by brightness. The roar of lunchtime traffic on the avenue abated to a hum and an occasional whirr.

"Hey, Marty. Look at this guy, come here." Quitman motioned Marty over to join him at the showroom window. "What the hell's that he's got on his feet?"

"Ostrich."

"What?"

"Ostrich-skin boots."

16

Playing the yokel Quitman said, "What'll they think of next, huh?"

"That's the kind you get when they run the 'miracle car' ad. I hate it when their ad's in the throwaways. It brings every roach in town out of the woodwork."

"You want him, Marty? Might stop your whining."

"You saw him first. You're stuck, O'Neil."

Quitman pushed through both double doors into the lot and started toward VanDyk.

VanDyk called to the lotboy, "Who was the guy just drove in in the Porsche?"

The kid turned his sullen brown eyes on him, "You mean Marty?"

"Yeah, Marty, I thought I recognized him. Thanks."

"How can I help you today?" Quitman said from ten feet away, striding toward VanDyk, hand already extended. "My name's O'Neil."

"Friends call me Bob."

Quitman felt no commitment in their handshake. Nothing tentative, but nothing sincere either. The glassy, dull brown eyes scratched a hollowness behind Quitman's sternum, next to his heart. "Can I call you 'Bob?'"

"Sure."

"I like those boots. Ostrich, aren't they?"

"Sure are."

"I didn't see you pull up, Bob. What kind of car you driving?" Quitman cast his eyes over VanDyk's shoulder, looking up and down the lot.

"Just an old heap. It's across the street," he said, gesturing vaguely in the air. "Is Marty here?"

"Sure is," Quitman said, a little disappointed at losing his shot at the rube, "I'll get him for you."

"It's just that I've talked to him before, a while back, and, well, you understand," VanDyk lied. He kept his hands moving as he spoke, hoping to keep the interest off his face and on his jewelry.

"He'll be right out."

"That was quick," Marty cracked when Quitman returned. "What'd he buy?"

"Fuck you, huh? He asked for you."

"Really?"

"Yeah. He asked if we had any salesmen that didn't know shit."

"Suck a rope."

"By name," Quitman said. "He asked for 'Marty.' "

"Not a roach after all. Could be my lucky day."

*

"You know, Marty," VanDyk began, sitting relaxed at the wheel of the big Lincoln, gliding it over the railroad tracks, "You showed me the trunk when we stopped back there but I don't remember, was there a spare?"

"Of course there was, Bob. Practically brand new. Whitewall. Just like the ones on the car."

VanDyk smiled. "Not one of those doughnuts, huh? A real tire? A jack, too?"

"Bob." Marty put his hand on VanDyk's arm, "Pull over, we'll look again."

"Right here?"

"Why not?"

"You sure, Marty? I mean, I believe you."

"Really. Let's look."

As VanDyk eased the car over by the loading docks alongside the road Marty dropped open the glove compartment door and hit the remote trunk release button.

"You got any hobbies, Marty?"

"Me? Like what?"

VanDyk threw the shift into park and looked over at Marty's plump face. "Like coin collecting."

"Nope," he answered, popping open the door. They walked to the rear of the car where Marty pointed and said, "See, Bob, there's the spare. And over here by the wheel well," he reached in and pulled back a small gray-felt curtain, "is the ja—"

VanDyk cut in saying, "I'm interested in coins, Marty."

"Me too. I like spending them," he said, giving a slight shrug.

"I mean in collecting."

"That must be interesting." Marty said, smiling, pausing a moment. What's with this guy, he thought. He tried to move the conversation back to business, "What do you think about the car, Bob? This Lincoln's a beautiful car. It says something positive about its owner. It suits you, you know."

VanDyk's brown eyes narrowed. "I don't care about the car, Marty. When I said I was interested in collecting maybe you misunderstood me. I meant that that's what I'm here to do, collect the coin. The silver dollar."

"What are you talking about, Bob? I thought you wanted to buy a car. What's this with coins? I don't know anything about a coin. I don't—"

The slap came out of nowhere, knocking Marty back against the car, banging his head on the open trunk lid. He grabbed his stinging skull with both hands and moaned. VanDyk seized Marty by the tie and jerked him toward him. Marty's eyes popped in their sockets, his face turned white, he sucked short gasping breaths. "What are you doing?" he shrieked. He struggled to wrestle himself free. The shirt ripped away from his neck. He tried to escape but VanDyk was too quick for him. Marty wailed a mournful *Please* as VanDyk spun him around and tossed him into the trunk.

"You're going to tell me about the coin! Tell me

now, while it can still do you some good!"

"But I . . ."

VanDyk reached into the trunk and grabbed a fistful of Marty's hair. He yanked him forward, "Stop whimpering, you fucking little cunt, I can't stand it when a man whimpers."

"But I . . ."

*

The plastic garbage bag made a dull thud when it hit the bottom of the empty dumpster. The bag tore slightly; through the opening peeked the toe of an ostrich boot. Hidden inside, the rest of the boot and its mate nestled among the false mustache and brown wig, the vest, cowboy hat, brown contact lenses, and western belt with the name "Bob" carved on its surface.

VanDyk considered himself in the rearview mirror, brushed a clump of blond hair from his broad forehead, then edged his IROC out of the alley and down the street.

Three

Henry Lyman reached both his large hands out and opened the double doors on the cabinet, revealing twenty-four drawers, each two inches high. He pulled the handle on the face of one and it glided open effortlessly, displaying the likenesses of kings and presidents, flora and fauna, ships and dreams etched through time into the present by the skills of engravers and minters, most long dead and forgotten. Most in mint condition, they lay in state on a sea of black velvet, shielded by glass; from the Willow Tree Threepence through the 1792 Silver Eagle.

VanDyk's entrance went unrecognized but not unnoticed. Lyman continued leisurely inspecting the coins. His eyes read the cases book-fashion, from left to right.

VanDyk suddenly opened the silence like a door. "What's a collection like that worth?"

"In terms of money?"

What else, VanDyk thought, but said instead, "Yes. In those terms."

"Quite a lot."

"I could've guessed that," he said, feeling perturbed at having to talk to Lyman's back.

"Money isn't the only consideration in terms of value," Lyman continued, turning toward VanDyk now, "Not by a long shot. I could tell you that my coin collection is worth several hundred thousand dollars."

He watched with delight as VanDyk's eyes sparked to attention like a watchdog's at a snapped twig. He poured a single brandy and sipped at the glass. When he got no reply, verbal or visual, he went on. "Ownership. Owning something that most other people could never have is better than money. And what's even better than that is owning something exclusive enough that even those who could afford it, and would want it if they could get it, can't get it because you've got it."

"Is that what the 64 D is all about?"

"That's what life is all about." A silence settled between them until Lyman asked, "What about the salesman?"

"Dead," VanDyk replied, without even a hint of venom in his tone. Just a fact, cold as his own blue eyes.

Lyman's bulging eyes drew narrow as a frog's. "How? And why, Mr. VanDyk?"

VanDyk poured his own drink, watching Lyman from the corner of his eye. He took his time, now that control had passed into his grasp. The knobby glass decanter chilled his fingers. The aroma of aged brandy rose up to him, deep with the richness of fermented grapes. "He was a coward. I think he died of fright. Anyway, I don't think he's who you're looking for."

Lyman's breathing slowed. The muscles around his eyes relaxed and his face resumed its placid quality. "And why not?"

For Lyman this death was nothing more than a weeding out of the unnecessary. The passion that stirred him was for the prize—and the chase. He felt a rush of rage at the thought of losing the trail.

"Like I said. I didn't really hurt him. Not really," he sipped his brandy, then rolled the stem of the glass in his fingers. "We pulled onto a quiet side street, behind an industrial building, over on the west end. I told him I wanted to see the trunk again, that I'd forgotten if there was a spare or not." He paused long enough to smile in pride at his cleverness. "So, I pulled over, I was driving then, and he took the keys and we went around behind the car. When he opened the trunk I started to question him. When he tried to run I threw him inside. I didn't hurt him. Not enough for him to die. But I smelled it. The fear on him. When I yanked him up his breath stank and I could smell he'd pissed his pants. I tell you, he's not who you were looking for."

"You said that. Tell me why."

VanDyk slumped into a chair and leaned forward, elbows on knees. The grinding of his teeth visible at his jaw. "Christ, Mr. Lyman, afraid as he was he'd have told me anything, can't you see that?"

"Perhaps."

"No perhaps about it. I know people. In situations like that, I know people."

"This is unfortunate."

Vandyk rose from the chair and walked to the window. His footfalls silent on the thick carpet. "Want my opinion?" he said over his shoulder.

"No," Lyman yelled. "You must learn to control yourself, Mr. VanDyk. You went after Hackett too soon. There's probably forty car salesmen at that place. They could swap cars all the time. Hackett could have pointed out the right person. He could have I.D.d him for you. What have we got now? The plate wasn't enough, just not enough."

VanDyk relished the ensuing silence and was glad to hear that the venom had left Lyman's voice when he continued. "No matter. But the trail at the car dealer is cold. Or so hot, it's cold. We need a new approach,"

Lyman said, pacing. He spun toward VanDyk. "We need to start from our last known fact."

"Which is?"

"Denver."

"Denver? What's in Denver?"

"Denver, Mr. VanDyk, is where the coin was minted."

"Is that what the 'D' stands for?"

"Yes."

"Denver. In 1964? Christ. That's a long time. A lot of silt settles over a trail in that amount of time."

"We have to start with what we know, not what we feel or guess."

"And what do we know?"

"That it must have gotten out with some employee. Someone who worked on it between the striking and the meltdown," Lyman was visibly agitated by his own line of thought. His hands flexed as his pacing quickened. He sensed the acrid ghost-odor of molten silver. "You see, Mr. VanDyk, the 64 D was to be the resumption of the minting of new silver dollars. The first true silver dollars minted in this country since 1935 in . . . San Francisco, I believe. At any rate, three hundred sixteen thousand coins were struck by the silver dollar standard of ninety percent silver. But the silver controversy that arose caused the government to have second thoughts." He waved his hand vaguely in front of his face. "And they ordered them melted down." His face grew sad, almost bewildered that anyone would do such a thing.

"Then what makes you think there is one? Even Hackett didn't actually see it," VanDyk pointed out.

"A number of things. One, why would a car salesman with no knowledge of coins even broach a subject like that? Two, salesmen tend to be rather concrete in their thinking, so we can assume that he's at least seen it. And three . . . " Henry Lyman paused, his eyes shining with a mystical light. "We would all like to believe that it exists, that such things exist, wouldn't we?"

VanDyk turned from the window, bored with the bland sunniness of the treeless street. "But what if he wasn't a salesman, what if a salesman just lent his demo to someone?"

"Our man is a salesman, I'm sure of it. But the salesman is irrelevant at this point. He'll still be there when we need him."

𝓕𝓸𝓾𝓻

He relished the sparkle in Maria's eyes when the light turned green, she popped the clutch and the hefty 2.5 liter engine of the tiny Fiero hurled them down the street. Maria's long chestnut hair furled free of its single barrette in the stiff breeze from the opened windows. He watched her short fleshy body as she glided the shift through the gears, her eyes fixed intently on the road.

"I love this car, O'Neil," she said.

"They're not making them anymore."

"All the better," she said, hitting sixty in second gear thirteen seconds past the light.

"You'll enjoy this car. Suits you. Fits like a glove."

"I even like the color, the red."

"Matches your nails."

"Thanks." She grinned.

"And your personality, I think."

"Thanks again." She paused, then continued, "I think," slipping into fourth. "It's a little pricey."

"In line with the market."

"I checked the Blue Book with the bank."

"There are other things to consider. When you're shopping Classics, the Book hardly counts."

Quitman loved used cars. He loved that it was impossible to shop them. Each car was a one-of-a-kind, a collectible if you sold it right. People had nothing to go on but the look on your face and the tone in your voice: Trust.

"I looked at an IROC down at Butler that I liked, too."

"Maria. Can I call you Maria?" She nodded. "Maria," he began again, "two things. No. Let me ask you this. If you liked it so much, the IROC at Butler, why didn't you buy it?" He rotated in the tight bucket seat to look directly at her profile. He knew that, since she was driving, she couldn't turn to look back at him, but he also knew she could sense his dark eyes, feel his warm breath brushing her cheek as he spoke.

"I wanted time to think."

"Know what I think? I think you didn't like it enough." He paused, waited for her to steal a glance at him, then he smiled. "Want to know what I also think?" Not waiting for an answer, he went on, "I think you do like this enough."

"Pretty sure of yourself."

"Sure of the product."

"I'm not sure I'll buy tonight. Don't get your hopes up."

The paperwork took just over an hour. Quitman admired the turn of her calf as she got back behind the wheel. He stuck the temporary permit to the rear window, shut the door, and waved good-bye as she drove the little red Fiero, the little red hunk of iron and rubber, over the curb torward home.

❦

As Maria was standing in her bathroom, leaning forward at the waist, he watched from the bed as she deposited her breasts into the cups of her bra, and while still bent forward hooked the four rear clasps. She then stood upright and with one hand held the bottom edge of the bra, along the stay; she used the other hand to gently shift the soft flesh above the cup until it felt comfortable.

She pulled on a robe and stood in the doorway brushing the dampness from her hair. "I swear, O'Neil, the next time I pass a beauty parlor I'm going to have something done with this hair." She tugged the brush through the final snarl with a wince and a tiny "ouch."

"What's the matter with it?"

"Snarly. It tangles all the time."

"Get it cut short."

"Don't you like my hair?"

Already regretting this conversation, Quitman sighed, "I think it's beautiful."

"But you'd like it better short?"

"I didn't say that."

"But would you?"

"Would I what?" He dragged his mental feet, hoping she'd give up.

"Like it better if my hair was short."

Exasperated. "Would you cut it if I did?"

"Depends." She lifted her hair from her neck and turned to consider herself in the bathroom mirror. "I don't think I'd look good with it short. Look at my ears. Do you think I have funny ears? They'd show all the time if my hair was short. What do you think," she said, coming full into the bedroom, "do I have funny ears?"

"Let's have a closer look." He began reaching his hand around to the nape of her neck and pulling her down toward him. He inhaled the soapy freshness of her skin. "They don't make me laugh," he whispered into one of the organs in question.

"Not now, O'Neil. I have to get ready."

"Me too, you know? Just a kiss then."

Her kiss was terse, distracted, obligatory. Quitman

felt an emptiness balloon in his chest. He watched her peel off her robe and wiggle into her dress. Even through the fabric, his senses still filled with her flesh and it occurred to him that under her clothes she was naked, tempting him. He closed his eyes to break the spell. "I want to get in early. See Marty get fired."

"Didn't he come back yesterday at all?" Maria didn't need to be reminded by the mirror to stand up straight. Her posture was naturally erect, her shoulders level and her arms strong.

"No, the crazy fuck. He took off about three on a demo-ride and that was it. No call. No nothing."

She disliked the swearing but she let it pass. "Maybe he broke down."

"Somewhere where there's no phone?"

"Yes."

"No such place, Maria. Not in this lifetime. He fucked the goat and he's going to get what's coming to him."

"I hate that kind of talk."

"It says what it means."

"I don't think it says anything. 'Made love to a goat,' really."

"I didn't say 'made love,' I said——"

"I know what you said; it's vulgar, that's all."

"Well, I want to be there when he gets whatever you want to call it, that's all."

"You're strange. O'Neil," Maria observed, stepping into her high-heeled shoes, making the transition from female to woman in front of Quitman's eyes. She appraised herself in the mirrored wardrobe door. She smoothed the fabric over her pelvis with her palms and said, "My hips look puffy. I need a diet. Do you think I need a diet?"

The blood in Quitman's veins slowed to the point of

lethargy at the thought of another conversation like the one about her hair. He declined to answer.

She undid the belt of silver medallions from around her waist and fluffed at her shirtdress. She was more satisfied with the unclenched look, the unaccented breasts and hips. "There," she said, walking over to him, "better without the belt, don't you think?"

"Better," he said, although when he thought about it he preferred the belt.

She leaned over and gave another distant kiss and said, "I'll pour you coffee and put out some toast. Be a hon and stick the dishes in the dishwasher before you go." Checking the contents of her purse she continued, "I know it's in here."

"What?" he asked, the raw aroma of freshly splashed perfume scratching at the inside of his nose.

"Here it is," she said, putting a key on the bedstand beside him. "Lock up, please. Just slide the key under the door. Call me later?"

"Sure," he said, and she was gone, though the memory of her scrubbed and scented body lingered in the air, fading slowly.

Quitman brought his coffee back to the bedroom. He opened the drawer in the bedtable: a bottle of aspirin, several romance paperbacks, hair curlers, a make-up mirror, breath mints, a curling iron, a pamphlet titled "Contraceptives and You," a handgun. The gun shocked him, made the hairs on the nape of his neck vibrate. He knew women owned guns. Trinket-types, little derringers with pearl handles or nickel-plated .25 automatics. But a Bulldog .45, with the bluing looking worn from loving use, was something else again. A little girl like Maria, he thought, who didn't like profanity and nearly cried every time she brushed out her wet hair after a shower. A girl who pouted when she saw her hips in the mirror kept a gun by her bed that could take off a grown man's head at twenty feet.

He shut the drawer and popped open the cabinet below, smiling at the mixed collection of women's magazines on fitness and health, and *Playgirls*. He fingered the Ben-wa balls and looked at, but did not touch, the dildo. He remembered as a child having found a dildo in his parents' room—red, white, and blue like the flag, remnant of the revolution, he chuckled to himself.

He clicked the cabinet shut and hit the button on the remote for the television. Sitting on the bed, he seesawed his tie under his collar and waited for the picture to come up. The screen grew light and the image burned on. The police cordon of yellow tape surrounded a white Mark VII. He lunged for the remote. His fingers fumbled trying to bring up the sound and the image changed. The voice came on, "And in other news. . . ." He jumped through the channels nervously, switching so quickly that he flashed past the Lincoln and had to fumble it back onto the screen. "The body of Jorgé Martinez was found early this. . . ."

"Fuck," he said.

*

A bald man in a checkered jacket, black slacks, and black-and-white shoes caught Quitman by the arm as he came through the agency door, "I been trying to call you. Don't you ever go home?"

"Nice to see you, too, Jerry."

"You heard?"

"I heard."

"What the fuck is the world coming to?"

"Dunno," Quitman said, studying the etched lines in Jerry's face, "I just don't know."

"The cops are coming here this morning. Want to

talk with everyone he worked with. Management says cooperate. Like we had a choice. It's too bad."

"About Marty?"

"About business. They kept saying 'West's Classic Auto Sales' all morning on the tube. Who's going to come here now? Shit."

"You're all heart, Jerry." I hope someday they find a cure for baldness and nobody tells you, he thought.

"They'll be here in a half-hour. Don't disappear."

Quitman made his way down the hall to the coffee room and plopped the two-dozen assorted on the counter.

"You hear, O'Neil?" Sal asked.

"I heard."

"Gangland-style they said. Jesus, gangland-style."

"I heard. He even asked for Marty by name."

"You talked to the guy? The guy Marty went on the spin with?"

"Yeah."

"I feel for you."

"Why?"

"You'll be looking at scumbags in mug books till your eyes fall out."

Quitman's eyes narrowed. His voice was honed to a fine edge, "I lost a partner, too."

"Yeah, yeah, that, too. I'm sorry," Sal said back over his shoulder as he walked out of the room.

Me, too, he thought as he continued to glare at Sal's back as he ambled down the hall.

The sales force assembled in the small terraced theater at the rear of the agency, the same one they met in on Monday mornings to hear the manager's speeches and watch the auto channel on cable to get themselves pumped up for the week. Quitman remembered when he started at West's. Marty brought him in that first morning. "The first row's for management, the second's for ass-kissers. Let's sit in the back," Marty had joked in a hoarse whisper. Quitman sat in the back this time as well, folding his jacket on the seat next to him, Marty's seat.

Up the hall, the other managers gathered around Jerry's desk. One of them said, "What should we do?"

"We need to come up with some kind of safety policy for when the guys go out on spins," another replied.

"Maybe we ought to close for a couple a days," another said.

Jerry slapped the top of his desk. "The owner would rip off my head and piss down my neck if I even mentioned something like that. What the hell's the matter with you people? Business as usual, as much as possible. Jesus. You want to look like we're hiding from something? Today and tomorrow, the managers take the turns, work the lot. Show some of these 'Quaking Nellies' that we've got for salesmen what selling's all about. We're open for business. Get it?"

*

Quitman and the detective sat in one of the tiny cubicles that circled the showroom floor.

" 'Bout my height, a little taller. Stocky. More muscular build than me," Quitman began. "Brown hair, beard and mustache, brown eyes, I think, I'm not sure, I think they were brown."

The detective's nappy hair glistened with dressing. He too was about Quitman's height, only a little shorter: 5'11". His speech rolled from his fleshy lips like a speech too often made, "What was he wearing? What do you remember?"

Quitman smelled the peachy aroma of the detective's hair, he could almost taste its juiciness. "Cowboy hat.

Big brim. Plaid shirt, leather vest, ostrich boots, a broad belt with the name Bob carved on the back. I saw it when he got in the car with Marty. Lots of jewelry. Pinky rings, turquoise belt-buckle—a real Halloween type, know what I mean?"

"Not exactly."

"Before I knew he wanted Marty, when I was walking out to him, I was qualifying him, preplanning, you know? I thought once we got started, after talking about the car, I'd talk about weight training, Nautilus, Merle Haggard, and Hank Williams, Jr. Loosen him up. Get his confidence. All I saw was style, no substance, understand? The guy was a 'Blow.' "

"A what?"

"A Blow, you know. A breeze. A vapor. Someone who's difficult to get a grip on. You talk to him and you feel his invisible hand on your chest, holding you at arm's length. Someone who's not even shopping. Just killing time. Just blowing through."

"He wanted Martinez particularly? Were you surprised by that?"

"Yes. He asked for him by name."

"Last name?"

"Nickname: Marty. He asked for Marty."

"Anything else?"

"Not offhand." As he took the detective's card, he looked into the lost eyes. He promised to call if he thought of anything else.

Quitman drank an hour's worth of bitter coffee, alone in his cubicle, watching the lot through the enormous windows. He watched the heat of an already hot day shimmer off the asphalt, the sun glinting off the chrome of those cars that had some. His body twitched internally from time to time, as though it anticipated something awful was imminent, an omen arriving after the event, startling him each time. He spun toward the phone to break the spell and keep his promise.

He called Maria's, though he knew she wasn't home. He got no comfort from her machine. "This is Maria. Do you like hearing my voice? I'd love to hear yours. I'll call, I promise." The machine beeped the solitary chirp of a sick bird.

Not tonight, he thought, and keyed in the combination for Helen Costello.

❡

Helen twirled the thermostat dial, kicking on the air conditioner, then struck a match to the gas log in the fireplace. They had both been silent since he'd arrived. Quitman lifted his wine glass from the ball-and-claw table in front of the sofa and sat on the floor, facing the fire. Helen threw down a second cushion and sat beside him.

"I talked to the guy that killed Marty," he said.

Her hand trembled below the surface of her skin. "Thank God you're safe."

"I don't feel very safe. What's the point?"

"Of what? The point of what, Quitman?"

"Anything. A guy goes to work and some weirdo kills him. What for? He didn't like the color of the car or what?"

"He asked for Marty, didn't he?"

"What's that supposed to mean?"

"Maybe it was something else," she pleaded. "Maybe Marty knew him from somewhere else?"

"He didn't recognize him. That's not like Marty." He ran both hands through his coarse hair. "That's not like any of us. We go to sleep at night dreaming about the people we talk to, for chrissake. Our whole business depends on getting people to keep the bullshit promises they make. We have to remember them or we starve. And Marty didn't remember this guy. This guy in a ten-gallon hat and plops on his feet."

"Shower shoes?" she asked, her face both a question mark and an exclamation point.

"No. Cowboy boots. You have to listen to them. When somebody walks by in them, they plop. They're flat-footed, everybody's step sounds the same. And he's got jewelry hanging on him like he's a rack in a department store. Who wouldn't remember him?" Quitman drank hard at his glass.

"All day today I knew he was dead." He paused, drank again. "I saw pictures of him dead. That's all we talked about all day, that he was dead. And every time I walked by his cubicle, I looked in. I even thought I could smell that lavender shit he wore all the time; the bath water." He filled his laugh with cynicism. Not purposely but from the embarrassment he felt. "He wasn't there. He shouldn't have taken the guy out so fast. He should've qualified him better. He was too fucking hungry. You shouldn't have spun him, Marty. You dumb Spic." He closed his eyes, held the lids tight. His saliva tasted of salt and clung to his tongue like glue.

"You don't mean that," Helen said, helpless to aid him. She moved to kneel behind him. She rubbed her warm hands along the sides of his neck. "It could have happened to anyone." This comforted neither of them.

"I don't want to think that," he said. "When my parents were killed—they were drunk; she was driving, I think, I don't know for sure, I just know what they told me—random in a way, but I could explain it. But this, Jesus. You like to think there's more to your life. That it couldn't be you. You have to think it, otherwise it's out of control, random. If he didn't die because he was dumb, then why did he? He had on the wrong tie?"

"They said on the news it was a gangland-style killing," she said, trying to provide rhyme or reason.

"That's another thing I never understood: underworld crime, gangland. What the hell are they talking about? The guy was some kind of freak. Gangland. Underworld. When I was a kid, I thought you could get there through a cave or something. I thought it was a place, like Disneyland or Coney Island. Can you imagine that? What a dumb kid; just like that dumb bastard Marty. Poor dumb Marty, too stupid to see the truth."

"Don't be so hard on him, Quitman. When my husband died, I felt some of the same things. You know what bothered me most?"

She turned and sat on the floor, resting her back against his. She stayed silent for a moment, the cusps of her eyes holding tears, then, "When Jimmy died, his sister, Margaret, came to Denver to help me. They lived here then," she added absently.

Quitman stared into the fire, watching the gas flame leap from the metal log like bright spires in the night. Helen's voice tolled like a distant bell in a fog, coming from nowhere and everywhere, melancholy.

"She answered the phone, made the calls, made the arrangements, did everything. The day after the funeral, she told me she had gone through Jimmy's things and had gotten some boxes ready for the Goodwill. I couldn't believe it. He was more of a man to me than that. Far more personal than that. I just suddenly felt like I could be sent to the Goodwill, too. Just another thing he had that was still useable, still had some life left in it. Another jacket or a pair of shoes or his electric razor, there I'd be, hanging on a rack or lying in a bin marked 'Widows.' They'd look at my face, my hair, under my dress." Her tears leaped her lashes drawing parallel paths across her cheeks; they dripped from her jaw to her lap.

"I dragged the boxes of clothes to the backyard and doused them with charcoal lighter and lit them. What was his would die with him. To this day I don't know why I didn't jump in. I wanted to. You don't know how I wanted to."

Quitman felt her back sobbing against his. "Helen," he said, turning toward her, "what's wrong?"

*

The blue-green webbing of the sling's strap chafed at Hackett's neck. On the drive to the cemetery, every time he wanted to shift the Volkswagen's gears, he had to stretch across and do it with his left hand, meanwhile having to keep the steering wheel steady with the bandageless fingertips of his right hand. The process was tedious and didn't go unnoticed by other drivers who took the opportunity to exercise their horns and their "fuck you" salutes. He scanned the several processions at the cemetery using the old Zeiss field glasses he'd had since childhood.

Emile Hackett was not a man who liked to bathe. His anorexic body frightened him: the sight of it, the feel of it. He avoided contact with it whenever possible. His senses seemed to have never fully developed. He wasn't drawn to the smell or taste or sight of food. He'd always been dangerously thin. Sitting in the airless, sweltering Volkswagen, working the binoculars with the wrong hand, he didn't even notice how much like an overripe bathroom hamper it smelled. Or how the gray steering wheel was mottled with a caked grime.

"So difficult to recognize anyone with everyone wearing such similar clothing," he murmured to himself. From his distance, the gatherings looked somber. Almost all the men in black, standing with their heads bowed. Who were they fooling? When was the last time they had a kind word for each other? He scanned the procession on the knoll under the elm. Then down the knoll, across a strip of curving concrete walk that glared, brightly magnified in his eyes by the field glasses, to a flat spot flanked by willows. He failed to recognize him at first. He lowered the glasses and massaged the bridge of his nose then raised the glasses again to the willows. "He's alive," Hackett proclaimed, locking the focus on Quitman O'Neil as he embraced Betty Martinez and then lifted Marty's daughter, Gloria, into his arms.

Quitman squinted at what seemed to be the brightest day he ever witnessed. He listened to the whirr of the conveyor lowering Marty's body into the ground and a blanket of claustrophobia dropped over him, shortening his breath to gasps—palpitating his heart. He felt last night's bourbon throb in his skull. He felt hollow and thin-shelled, unfortunate. His skin tingled with nerve pulses like worms crawling over his flesh. He longed for an external force to keep him from imploding, collapsing in on himself. Since getting out of the car and walking to the grave, he'd sweated enough to drench his shirt and dampen his suit jacket. The combination of the blaring sun and last night's bourbon made every pore in his body leak. Even the slight breeze gave him a chill and he had to consciously refrain from urinating in his pants. He was woozy with dehydration; a putrid taste he couldn't swallow clung to the back of his teeth. The lush grass looked like the best bed he could imagine and he wished he could lie down on it, even just for a moment.

Three other car salesmen showed up along with Jerry Stein, the G.M. Quitman crossed the asphalt path to where Jerry stood, leaning against the fender of his White Jaguar with the vanity plate that read "1WHTKAT." He was bent forward wiping the dew and dirt from his blue patent-leather shoes that were a head-on color match for his sharkskin suit.

"I'd have thought there'd be more people," Quitman said when he got close enough to be heard.

"You're young, kid."

"I'd 've thought West would have told more of management to come. Marty was in the Millionaire's Club three times over, for chrissake. He made them a fortune."

Jerry straightened. He refolded his handkerchief so that clean surfaces faced out and wiped at some imaginary spots on the driver's window. "If I hadn't come on my own," he began, then, gesturing toward the salesmen standing fifteen feet from them, "and dragged that handful of misfits with me, you'd be standing here staring at the horizon, instead of my beautiful face."

"The fuck's with people, Jerry? The hell ya got to do to them to make them feel? And before you say what you're going to say, why the hell don't you know?" Quitman looked up, turned half away, looked down, squeezed the bridge of his nose trying to cancel the tears.

He heard Jerry's car door click open. "You want to go for a drink, kid? Might help."

Quitman, sensing for a moment, as he had when his parents died, that the roots of grief ran deeper than the roots of his, or any other, language, fought to smile. "Some other time."

*

"Mrs. Lizabeth Martinez?"

"Yes. This is Betty. Who's this?" she said, sitting on the bed by the phone, kicking off her shoes, crossing her legs, massaging one foot. "Who? I'm sorry, I can't hear you. There are people here, you'll have to speak up. Oh, wait a minute, hold on." She called to her daughter, "Gloria, Gloria. Come and close the door."

The little girl came running down the hall, looking like a communion angel whose outfit had been dipped in black. She stopped motionless in the doorway. "Close the door for Mommy," Betty urged. The girl put her hand on the knob but made no other move. "Please, Gloria. For Mommy. I'll be right out, I'll give you some cake, I promise." Gloria backed up, taking doorknob and door with her. "I'm sorry. I can hear you now. Who is this?"

"This is Mr. Fentor," Lyman lied, "and I'd like to express my deep sorrow at the loss of your husband."

"Thank you. Did you work with Marty? I don't recognize your name."

"No, Mrs. Martinez. And I hope you don't consider this call inopportune but I understand your husband had a coin collection."

"Marty?"

"Yes. And some of them might be quite val—"

"Marty? Coin collection? Is this a joke?"

"Far be it for me to joke at a time like this—"

"A coin collector. Marty spent them faster than he got them. I don't think this is funny," she shouted, banging the phone into its cradle.

The air in the house lay under the spell of the Mexican buffet that the mourners helped provide. The flighty aroma of cilantro wove the scents of crushed tomatoes and cracked pepper together.

Quitman looked in the kitchen for Betty. He wanted to leave, go rest his head. The bubbling pots on the stove added to the heat of the day. Jesus hung from his cross on the wall behind the stove, overseeing the inferno. Some of the thousand or so little children, at least that number seemed right, used his legs to hide behind or swing around as they did their best to stave off boredom.

Quitman saw Betty come around the kitchen doorway. She stopped to talk with her sister. As he approached, he overheard her answer her sister's question with, "I don't know. Some weirdo talking about coins."

"Wait a second," Betty said when Quitman made his excuses, "I want you to take Marty's stuff, you know, his briefcase, the little card file."

"Why?"

"It's just names of people he'd met. You know, that wanted cars. He'd want you to have it, don't you think?" Her tone was dazed, artificial with control.

Though Quitman had no use for it, he smiled and kissed her cheek. "I don't know if he would or not, but I'd like to have it."

☙

Lyman folded the obit clipping and methodically shredded it between his fingers.

"It appears you're right, Mr. VanDyk, it appears you're right."

He rose from his desk and paced to the window. Staring out into the brightness he rubbed his dense-hooded eyes. "A poet said it best; he said, 'A thing of beauty is a joy forever and can never fade into a money-making nothingness.' I want that coin."

VanDyk rose from the sofa at the far end of the room, put down his wine glass, brushed the constantly errant strand of blond hair from his forehead and asked, "Denver then?"

"To Denver."

☙

Putting Marty's card file and briefcase on the car seat beside him, Quitman thought of Maria. He thought of Helen. Neither thought satisfied. He went home alone.

In the two-room darkness of his condo, his pulse slowed, his breathing grew rhythmic. He flipped his dark glasses onto the scatter of open and ignored mail on the counter. He swallowed a greedy gulp of last night's bourbon. He walked into the living room and dropped his jacket on the always-open hide-a-bed, where it conformed to the rumpled covers.

He sat on the bed, looking into the darkness, rehearing the voice of Detective Jackson Fresh, visualizing his earthy lips precisely forming words, "Wanted to check back with you. See if something new might have popped into your head."

"Something's been bothering me since we talked and I couldn't tell what it was, but now I know. He didn't have a drawl. Most people dressed like that have some kind of drawl," Quitman had said, "Certain patterns go with the clothes. Overly polite, rowdy. You know, that 'Yes ma'am' and 'Howdy Partner' crap? It wasn't there, no twang, no nothing. He was a businessman."

"You think it was a disguise?"

"I dunno. Aren't they all?"

Fresh had fixed him with a bored stare. Large brown pupils in a sea of yellowish-white. "You know what I mean."

"I know what you mean, but I dunno. Shopping the big ticket's different. It's an event. People dress up for it. They psych up for it. They got it all laid out in their head just what's gonna happen, even down to what you're gonna do. I mean, the salesman. It's like they're in a movie or they're a gladiator or something. Put on your power clothes and go kill the lion. I just don't know."

"Would tie in with the gang idea."

"Why would a gang be after Marty?"

"It's usually one of three things: Drugs, money, sex."

"You mean he could've just fucked the wrong girl?" Quitman had bowed his head, shaking it in a gesture of disbelief.

"Did he have a bookie?"

Silence.

"Would you tell me if he did?"

"I don't think he did. Not in any serious sense. Everybody bets now and then."

"Was he chronically broke?"

"We're all chronically broke. What've you got in the bank?" Quitman had snapped.

Fresh sprang to his feet, squaring off in front of him. "I'm really thin on your bullshit. Just answer the questions and save the fucking editorials for the fucking cocktail hour."

Quitman had locked eyes with him and let the silence fill the space around them. Neither flinched. "Not anymore broke than the rest of us, which sounds like the same answer to me. You got certain phrases you want me to use, let me know." He had smiled as sarcastically as he could—at least he hoped it looked sarcastic and not stupid, defiant and not lame. "We both want the same thing, right?"

When he saw the muscles in Fresh's jaw relax, he knew the sarcasm had worked. He gave silence another brief run.

"Right."

"So?"

"So, Marty drank a little, smoked a little dope as a teenager, but he was down on drugs because of what's been happening to kids lately—and sex, Marty'd fuck a tree if there was nothing else around. It was like a hobby. People don't kill each other for that anymore, do they?"

"Where've you been?"

"I dunno," a common answer for Quitman these days. Where had he been anyway, he wondered?

"If it was vengeance, reprisal, vendetta, something like that," Fresh had gone on, "someone involved might show up at the cemetery. Maybe even the killer himself, out of a sense of personal or professional pride."

"Sick."

"They like to see the damage they've caused. The family. The friends."

Breathing.

"All I ask, keep your eyes open, that's all. Anybody you don't recognize, even outside the immediate area. At another grave nearby maybe, or by the cars, wherever."

"Why don't you just go?"

"This isn't the only case I'm working on."

"That's a comfort. You guys are like doctors, if we haven't solved the problem ourselves, before we come to you, you're pissed," Quitman said, as he had turned his back on him.

After that conversation, Quitman had started on the bourbon, determined to see nothing the next day, but it had only made things worse, flooding his veins with adrenaline. Everyone had looked guilty to Quitman, everyone capable. Even Marty's ex-wife and five-year-old Gloria, his daughter, had conspiracy in their oval, Keene-like eyes. No one had cried. No one looked sad enough. The priest referred to a three-by-five card wedged in his prayer book when he needed Marty's name. People whispered, even during the prayers. Most of the women seemed oblivious to the fact that they manufacture different perfumes for daytime and night-time. And none of the men, except him and the priest, had seemed to own a suit.

Quitman slurped the last of a double from his glass. Being alone wasn't the answer.

Five

Maria stepped backward from her final repetitions on the stair climber and kept going until she came to the gym's indoor walking track where she began her usual two laps walking backward on the imitation gravel surface. She felt it improved her coordination and helped her muscles to unwind more fully than walking forward. She'd never found a trainer who would agree or disagree with it but everyone found it novel. It was more difficult and less funny than it appeared. It required most of her concentration. She navigated by keeping a lane line between her feet.

She had exercised most of her life. In fact she had trained ever since she could remember, and probably before that. Her father must have had her doing something that would be good for a future world-class gymnast to do, even in her crib. Most likely when she reached out and grasped his fingers he expected her to pull herself forward a certain number of times.

Her shoulders were straight and sloped like a wrestler's, and her arms and legs were long and sinewy like a swimmer's. These characteristics gave her excellent advantage in floor exercises, parallel bars, and rings. She was strong and graceful, her carriage had the beauty of sureness to it. She garnered medals, trophies, and plaques from the time she was four years old. She was Olympic material, everyone agreed, a shoo-in for the gymnastics team.

She was fourteen and acne nearly covered her face and back. She trained three hours a day in the morning before school and four hours in the late afternoon. The competition was stiff, she had to be ready. But the real competition came from within. All the exercise and work had stalled the ticking of her biological clock or reset it, as it will, until, one day, during a dismount from the bars, her abdomen contracted into a cramp that yanked her into a knot and dropped her hard on her hip, cracking her ilia in a painful hairline web that radiated from the helix.

The timing couldn't have been worse, her father told her. As though she controlled the fall. As though she had somehow orchestrated that awkward flip through the air as a new part of some routine. She'd never be back on her feet in time for trials or in time for the preliminaries in Europe in the spring. She could though, she pleaded, train and be ready for the next time, daddy. She would. Promise.

During her convalescence, when she was no longer able to exercise, her body clock leaped forward in a catch-up-sprint and her puberty began with a vengeance. Her hips and breasts erupted her into womanhood, in what seemed like, to her, overnight. Almost as quickly, her constant companion from morning to night, her father, withdrew from her side and her mother was moved in in his place. He had known who she was before this happened, before this explosion of identity; why was it so different now? She was not so different now, not the real she, not the Maria who worked so hard to be right, to be the right Maria, with the right attitude and the right talents. The right Maria for the right daddy; what was so different now? What compelled him to formality where familiarity had once prevailed? What drove him to be gracious when a little rough-house would be so much more satisfying? What could she ever do to make things right again? How could she reverse the ticking clock and get him to notice that she was still there?

At the end of her counter-clockwise circuits it took her a moment to feel comfortable walking forward again. In the center of the track was the gym area with the equipment. A few of the other regulars said hello to her as she sat on a painted wooden bench to rest.

❧

"Hello."

"How was it?" Helen asked Quitman as he entered her house.

"Sad. The usual, you know?"

"Were there many people?"

"You have any bourbon?" He sat down heavily, sinking into the soft couch cushions.

"Mixed with anything?"

"Neat. . . . A couple of dozen people. His family, some friends from before, mostly people he worked with in the past. Salesmen." He rose to his feet. He looked around for whatever it was that he should have been doing but he couldn't figure out what that might be. "Jerry, the G.M., Some girls he'd laid." He spoke distractedly.

"Quitman," she reproached mildly.

"What?"

"Nothing. Here's your drink."

He frowned at the glass, at Helen. "Bring the bottle, will you?"

"It's no answer, Quitman."

He looked down into her face. The top of her head came to his chin.

"I'm not looking for an answer right now. I'm not looking for anything right now, except maybe a bigger glass or the bottle, okay? For now?" Her eyes took the brunt of his abruptness and blinked. "Please?" he added in condolence.

The bottle clicked glass-bottom to glass-top as she placed it on the table in front of him. "How about something to eat? It's the least you can do for your stomach lining."

The salt crystals from the first nibble of cracker set off an explosion of taste inside his mouth, the way they do if you haven't eaten in a long time. Suddenly everything smelled delicious. It shocked him to discover how hungry he was. The salami was rich with virgin oils, pepper, and fennel. The crackers held that tan-toward-brown odor of fresh baking, of being snatched from the oven's mouth without a second to spare. The cheeses reeked tantalizingly like a sudden whiff of pipe smoke picked up in passing. He hunched his tall narrow frame over the tray and neither spoke nor looked up until he was done.

Cracker crumbs and a spoiled napkin littered the once full tray before him. His stomach pushed tight against his skin. Helen looked at him, the profile of his face, the inset of the eyes, under the orbit of the brow, the brooding at the corners of his mouth. The way the seams of his shirt sat along his shoulders. The open collar where the "U" of his clavicle peeked out. The listless way his small-for-his-size hands lay in his lap. Her arms yearned to hold him, to comfort him. She held herself in check, torn, guilty at her selfishness, ashamed of her guilt.

"Feel better?" she asked, reaching over to the back of

his neck and working her fingers upward until they all but disappeared into his dark hair.

He looked into her open face. The eyes without restraint. The cheeks and jaw kindly set. Having just this morning stared into the face of death, the light from Helen's eyes kindled his lust as nothing had ever done before. He reached for her as she reached for him. Their fingers collided and a small giggle escaped them both. An embarrassed flutter flicked her eyelids. The bittersweet taste of bourbon rubbed over her tongue as their teeth clicked together. She grabbed him hard, yanking him over her. Her top tore at the shoulders when he jerked down at the neckline. He lunged for succor at her bared breast. Her hands worked frantically at the buttons of his shirt, ripping free those that wouldn't surrender. She squirmed out of her own underwear and unhooked his belt with a tug. She pulled her legs up and hooked her toes over his waistband to drive his pants down to his knees. The fiercer his bite, the tighter her grip. He drew his face up to hers and she guided him.

She lay skewed, her upper body flat and her bottom half, knees together, turned on her left side. The dislodged hairs from his chest were clinging to the sweat on hers. Quitman opened the zipper on his pants and pulled them over his nakedness. He drank the neglected glass of bourbon, filled it, and drank it again. She reached her hand up to him. He caressed it gently at first, then clasped it in his and stepped back, pulling. Her knees thumped the floor. She scurried to her feet and followed his tugging hurriedly down the hall. She picked up speed. Got ahead of him at the bedside. She stopped, letting his body thump into hers. They fell back on the bed. They spoke in chuckles and grunts as they worked themselves onto the bed. Her arms were thrown up over her head. She used her hands, pressed flat against the oval wooden headboard, to respond to his thrusts by pushing back at him.

Her head nested on his chest, his hand rested on her back. She drew spirals on his belly with a fingernail.

"I've never felt . . ." she trailed off, confused. She had always thought of herself as making love. Never once had she penetrated the smooth surface of that facade and tasted its raw underbelly, not before this, not until now.

"What were you going to say?"

"I've never felt like I'd been . . . I mean . . . I've just never felt like this before."

"Like what?"

"How do you feel?" she said, hoping for some help.

"Hungry. Is that it? You're hungry?"

"Don't just change the subject like that," she said, hurt a little. "Won't you tell me how you feel?"

"I wasn't changing the subject. I am hungry." He eased her toward him. "Can I make something, get it for us?"

He studied her face. Those lines at her eyes, those pinches at her mouth; how very different they looked to him now, how precious they looked to him now, how they warmed him. He took her face in his hands and kissed each eye at its outside corner. He kissed her pale soft lips on each side, then in the center.

She snuggled down to rest her head on his chest. She took a playful, almost childlike tone, "If I feed you, will you tell me later?" She lifted her head and kissed his chin.

He held her tight. "I'll do better than that. I'll tell you now." She pressed her ear against his chest like an eavesdropper at the secret door. In a voice deep with relish he said, "I'm glad to be alive!"

*

Helen slept late the next morning. She rolled to the far side of the bed and absorbed Quitman's scent from his pillow as she had grown accustomed to doing. Even as she rose, her hand lingered in the indentation from his head.

The coffee Quitman had made before he left was beginning to turn bitter by the time she poured her first cup. The slip of oil in the cup rocked gently as she carried it to the living room and placed it on the desk. The room remained as it was last night: couch cushions on the floor, crumbs on the coffee table, a ravaged pizza box gaping by the fireplace. So that's what he meant when he said he'd fix something for the both of us to eat: Pizza. She smiled again at the thought of it. "Don't get up," he'd said, "I'll do dinner." Then he picked up the phone, and while it rang, he turned to her and asked, "Pepperoni okay?"

Lazily she turned the swivel chair to face out into the room and sat down. Her fingers felt comfortably warm clasped in her lap. Her gaze drifted around. She felt no burning urge to rearrange things, no desire to undo yesterday, no sense of insult to her pride, no urgency to the task. She inventoried, a this-can-stay, that-should-go survey of a room she hadn't bothered to notice much in the past five years. She rotated the chair to face the desk. Inside the top right drawer, her fingers poked idly through the pens and pencils, the adhesive-backed return address labels, the miscellaneous pins and clips. In the lower drawer, she found framed sets of coins and a pocket badge that read, "James Meyers, Quality Control

Supervisor, Dept. of the Treasury." She polished its face back to brightness with the corner of her robe and gently slid it into the pocket of her robe, amid the Kleenex. She lifted out the coin sets—each a perfunctory gift given to employees of his level and above at the start of a new minting—and thought, "These I'll keep." She glided the drawer shut, silent.

She dialed the phone. The Goodwill would come at four to pick up the desk.

She lifted a cushion from the floor and held it in her arms, lost for a moment, even to herself. Her pace quickened with each step to the bedroom. She flung open the wardrobe door. Her eyes danced across the dresses and slacks, blouses and tees, and skimmed the shoes and purses, belts and scarves. A dozen at a time, the clothes were draped over the bed, moved and sorted, mixed and matched. She dumped the contents of her jewelry into the pile. She dressed and undressed, accessorized and reaccessorized. She posed for the full-length mirror. Pouted and smiled. Gazed with lust and depravity. Framed her face with scarves and took on an air of divinity. She laughed out loud at some of the things she still had hanging around. She carefully rehung the things she liked, flinging the rest into a mound by the door.

Helen crammed the pizza box atop the gas log and lit it with a long, slender wooden match. Smoke billowed from the cardboard seams of the pizza box till the top *Ppuusshed* into flames, spewing a flash of light across her face and throughout the room.

*

The derelict-looking driver loaded the fifteen polybags of clothing. The clanging jolt of the hydraulic liftgate engaging gave Helen a start and she watched, with her mouth slightly open, as it lifted the desk and its contents

54

into the air. She stood on the sidewalk with arms crossed, one hand's fingers splayed across her upper chest, watching the big silver truck with the bright yellow letters turn the corner and disappear.

Six

Jackson Fresh was the kind of cop who still preferred the feel of his data on paper over the icy image of the computer screen. He disliked the insecurity he felt around floppy disks with their mysterious flimsy black covers and their megabytes of data that could suddenly disappear without a trace. That was one case he never wanted to have to solve. Since the computer had landed on his desk he often felt that the battle had shifted dramatically from one of good against evil to one of good against information. A neverending flow of largely meaningless data gushed across his desk, more than he could ever hope to read, much less absorb. He missed using his instincts, flying by the seat of his pants. Instead of the crush of men in the squad room discussing cases, investigations had turned into a roomful of women staring at computer screens all day. Instead of detectives lunching out of deli deliveries, there was a gaggle of uniformed coeds who went shopping at lunchtime and giggled in the coffee room during breaks.

He'd gone over the evidence a thousand times. At least his reddened eyes burned as if he had. The reams of fanfold paper on his desk were slashed through with black marker, eliminating the rereading of useless information. He looked around the room. His desk was the only one whose piles of papers threatened avalanche. All the others were neat and free of debris. Many were ornamented with plants or photographs or examples of private skills like crocheted sleeves for pencil holders and needlepoint samplers that said "Have a Nice Day."

"Got a minute, Fresh?"

He looked up into the face of the Chief of Homicide. "Sure."

"Come in then, will you?"

Fresh grabbed his bulging briefcase and followed Stevenson down the aisle, between the rows of moveable partitions and moveable walls, to his office.

"Some coffee, Jack?" Stevenson asked, gesturing to the pot on the credenza.

Fresh looked over the cups. Not one lacked a motto of some kind. "Our work begins when yours ends" was the latest homicide slogan. It showed a picture of a detective standing over a corpse. There were several of those. He declined. "Just had some, thanks."

"How's everything, Jack?"

Preliminaries, he hated them. "Fine. How about you?" hoping for a similarly terse reply.

"Fine. Splendid. Don't know if I've mentioned it or not, but my daughter's going to U.C. in the fall. Vivian and I are very happy about that. She was undecided for so long, she had us worried. Things are turning out for the best, though."

His daughter, Fresh thought, why didn't he just call her by name? Fresh had known her since the day she was born. Was this just another brick in the wall between the chief and himself? "I'm glad to hear it," he said.

Fresh and Stevenson had been close when they first came to this department. They'd landed there within two months of each other, recruited directly from college. "Phys Ed at Temple, huh? Why police work?" Stevenson had asked. Fresh had answered, "Blood runs through it." Stevenson glowed in that answer. He knew intuitively what Fresh had meant. He too had visualized police work as hot from its own coursing pulse. Alive. What they found, however, was good money for easy work. Command saw them as eager beavers, thorns that needed dulling; pains-in-the-ass. They called themselves the Rainmakers. When they were on an assignment things happened. Woe be to any supervisor too lazy to keep up, or so they thought. But soon Stevenson, with a wife and child to consider, saw a bigger picture of advancement and security. In that picture the Rainmakers idealism seemed petty and carping. Something that constantly battered itself, bruised on the iron framework of the bureaucracy.

"Children seem to need much more motivation these days," Stevenson was saying. "Sometimes it's difficult to identify the right button to push, if you know what I mean."

"Did you try her belly button?"

"Belly button?" Stevenson looked puzzled for a moment. "Oh, I see." He laughed politely. "Vivian will get a kick out of that, Jack, she surely will." He stopped, seeming to rethink what was just said, wondering whether to be offended, as he circled around his desk to take a position in his chair. "Can you update me on the Jorgé Martinez investigation?"

"Not much to tell."

"Gangs?"

"Don't think so."

"Why?"

"Just what I feel."

"We need more than that."

"Why do it at his job? Seems too risky for a gang. The killer met him face to face. That's not gang stuff. Gangs shoot people from moving cars. They're scared shitless of their victims. Afraid someone might snatch 'em up and spank their little asses. This wasn't a shoot-and-scoot. This was more than little-boy pride." Fresh leaned back in his chair, lifting the front legs off the floor.

Stevenson resisted the urge to ask him to sit up right. "Organized crime maybe? Make him an example?"

"Of what? An example of what?"

"Of what could happen. Maybe whatever was going on was going on at work."

"No sign of it. No drugs. No heavy gambling. He did like women. Why drive him away from there?"

"Frighten everybody else."

Fresh let the chair come forward, "I still don't see it."

"What about friends there? Anyone he was close to?"

"His partner, if you call that close. They socialized only rarely. Usually just saw each other at work."

"What'd . . . ah—"

"O'Neil. Quitman O'Neil."

"Unusual name. What did he have to say?"

"Said he didn't have a clue. Just that he talked to the murderer and thought his clothes were some kind of disguise, that he was trying not to be recognizable, incognito."

"A grudge, then?"

"Maybe, but not likely. That makes killing him on the job even more absurd. No, this guy killed him on the job because he didn't know where else to find him. He might not have even known who he was looking for."

"That doesn't make any sense to me, Jack, none at all. I'm considering turning this over to the computer people. Let them investigate by networking. Get it out of our bailiwick, out of our count."

Jack stood and faced the glass partition, looking on

the rows and columns of desks, the rows and columns of plants and samplers, his own reflection in the glass. He lifted his head a little so his chin wouldn't sag so much. He tucked at his shirt, sucked in his stomach, turned away from his reflection. Is that all it is, numbers, a count? he thought. "Let them. But let me, too," he requested.

"For how long?"

"For a while."

Stevenson swivelled his chair and got up facing a wall of framed diplomas and photographs. Among them was a mirror with a printed border that read DADDY OF THE YEAR. Finally he said, "Not a lot of time on this one."

"Not a lot."

"What will you pursue?"

"Dunno. O'Neil, most likely."

"You said they weren't close."

"I said," he paused momentarily, putting his hands into his pockets, "that he said 'they weren't close.' I'd like to see for myself."

Fresh returned to the squad room and asked uniformed Sergeant Billinski for help. "Alicia, I need some information on this man." He slid a folder from his rupturing briefcase and opened it before her. "Quitman O'Neil. Run down some records for me?"

Billinski's blonde hair, cropped short, hugged her head. She had broad, strong hips and legs, erect shoulders and a large chest. Her dark-blue uniform coupled with an impish grin made her appear less massive than she actually was. "Glad to help. Like what? Does he have a record?"

"No, not that I know of. No. I.R.S., Social Security; get me a picture from the driver's license section, would you? Get what you can. And some of what you can't, if you could, you know?"

She winked, but then frowned and said, "Take a day or so. The computer's down."

Fresh grinned.

Seven

Quitman looked at the calendar. "In the ground three weeks today. Happy Deathday, Marty, you poor dumb bastard," he said to himself. He snatched up the newspaper outside his door and took it to the rumpled bed where he sat to read by the light streaking through the blind.

Business had been good. Marty's death had an effect opposite to what everyone had feared. It brought people in droves. He'd had an outrageous offer on the white Lincoln, even took a deposit. Who cares why they come; once they're here we can sell them, Quitman thought.

He read through the paper. Killings with knives, guns, ice picks have fallen out of favor with murderers, but straight razors were making a comeback among the bar crowd. He read of the rape of an eighty-year-old woman by a teenager who had broken into her house. What'd they mean by rape, he wondered. Sex by consent was difficult enough, but sex by force can't even be sex at all. At least not sex as he thought of it. He kept trying to push the image of it out of his mind. "That kid must be a real drooler," he said to himself, and that helped a little.

He did the crossword, stuck on "21st state," trying to remember what it was, 16 down.

He called Maria and listened to her message. She changed it often but there was always one sure thing: Whatever the message was it was positive and upbeat. But he had nothing positive or upbeat to say in return. He listened to the hollow silence that followed the beep for several seconds before he just hung up on her machine.

Not much to see on his walls. He wasn't one to hang pictures or to even notice that pictures weren't hung. In a house like Helen's where details like that were attended to, he experienced a feeling of calm, of wholeness. He stared at the ceiling where it met the wall in a dim corner. The white pebble finish held only what his mind could provoke. On the uneven surface, images of monkeys danced and carcasses of forgotten dreams played in the light and subtle shadow. He always wished he could draw or paint the images his mind conjured in the seemingly meaningless patterns of bumps or cracks or stains. His mind would drift and he'd lose the image and not be able to find it again, sometimes not even remember what the image had been.

The knock on the door didn't stir him. It was the second or third pounding that finally got him to his feet.

"I've left messages on your phone."

"A phone's like a window, Fresh," Quitman said, stepping aside, gesturing for the cop to enter.

Fresh lifted his cap with two fingers and scratched his head with the remaining three. "I wish I cared what you meant by that, another time, maybe."

"Another time."

"I been following you," Fresh told him.

"Didn't they use to call it 'shadowing,' or something like that?"

"Cut it out."

"What?"

"Just answer the questions."

"What are you talking about? I didn't hear you ask any questions."

"I been following you, that's what I'm talking about. That's what I'm here to tell you."

Quitman yanked the blind open and drenched the room in light. Squinting, still facing the window, he felt the light hit the tops of his cheeks and the ridge of his brow, making them ache like they did when he ate ice cream too fast. He pinched the bridge of his nose, clamped his eyes shut tight, moistening them, and said, "Why?"

"It's my job."

He turned toward Fresh. "Get out of my house."

"We got a problem?"

"You're not going to get out of my house, is that it? You have a right to be here, that's what you're trying to tell me?" He waited, not really expecting an answer, not really expecting Fresh to leave. Then he said, "Why'd you follow me?"

Fresh laid his bulging briefcase on the opened hide-a-bed. It looked at home there. "Standard procedure."

"Procedure? That's the fuck you're telling me?"

"I had to make sure you weren't involved."

"That's a polite phrase," Quitman said, turning toward the lieutenant, "Involved. You're standing here, in my house, telling me you've been following me. I don't know why I let you in. I don't know what this is about."

"It's about Martinez, that's what it's about. Your friend, remember?" Fresh leveled.

"You been following me for that? What's your problem? Can't find the guilty, so you find the convenient?"

"Look, asshole," Fresh shot, "I'm just about done with your smart-ass humor."

"Yeah?"

"Yeah. Everything leads somewhere, even you. At least I thought so. That's what I came to tell you."

"That I lead nowhere. I already knew that. You could have just asked," Quitman said, pushing past Fresh toward the kitchenette. "What I don't know is who killed Marty. And, I gather from this, neither do you." The meaning of it suddenly struck him. "You know, Jackson, you know what following me seems like? It seems like you're covering incompetency with activity. Scurry around enough and people'll think you're doing something."

"I've heard this before," Fresh said, his voice measured and weary. "You don't understand my job."

No, Quitman didn't understand the job that confronted Fresh, not in the slightest. But looking at him now, standing there in his off-the-rack suit and rumpled shirt, the bottom button open, appearing suddenly very tired, Quitman understood that. His tone lightened. "Did following me help? You gonna catch the guy?"

"Dunno."

"What are your chances? What's the possibility you'll ever find him?"

"Not good without more to go on," Fresh said, lighting a cigarette.

"This is a new age. You're supposed to ask if you can smoke in someone's house."

"Do you mind," Fresh sneered, extending the cigarette.

Quitman smiled at the cracks in Fresh's veneer. "I don't mind," he said, plopping an ashtray on the clutter of mail, "I don't mind at all." He snapped open the top on a can of beer, and gestured it toward Fresh. "Ten A.M. too early for you?"

Fresh hesitated, leery for a moment, studying Quitman's face. The hostility was gone from the eyes, the mouth calm and relaxed. "No," he said, reaching for it.

"Bud okay? S'all I got."

"Bud's fine."

"So I'm innocent as far as you're concerned?"

Fresh sipped the foam off the can top. "Never thought you were guilty. You see," Fresh paused, pointing his finger casually at Quitman, "that's the part you don't understand: Protocols. I work from different assumptions than the constitution. I'm not a fucking Supreme Court justice, I'm a cop. I just thought maybe you knew something that even you didn't know you knew."

"Did I?"

"Not that I can see. The only thing you're guilty of is never coming home." Fresh jolted a mouthful of beer. The cold gurgling liquid tingled his nicotine coarsened throat. He closed his eyes in the pleasure of it. Then he said, "By the way, you know who Maria is?"

"My Maria? I mean the one I see?"

"Yeah, that one."

"Who?"

"My boss's daughter."

"Her father's a cop?"

"This is a new age." Fresh grinned. "How do you know it's not her mother who's the cop?"

Quitman smiled, sighed relief; he felt now that he understood the gun by Maria's bed. Second nature to her, he thought. He drained his beer, looked over at Fresh. "Another?"

"Why not."

"I suppose that helped clear me, the Maria connection?" he asked, handing Fresh his second beer.

"No. But it did make me think a little more kindly toward you. I've known her all her life. Think the world of her."

"We're just friends if that's what you're wondering."

Eight

No. I don't want any visitors," Helen had told him. "It's just a simple operation, a women's thing," she'd said.

"Why ninety miles away?" he had asked.

"That's where the specialist is." Her eyes grew wide. "You're not worried about me, are you? How sweet. Come sit by me, I want to hold you." She embraced him, squeezing gently. "Will you miss me, baby?" she had asked. "It'll only be two weeks."

He said he would do it so he did. Everyday after work, the time depended on which shift he was working, he stopped by Helen's house. He'd pick up the newspaper, bring in the mail. He flipped it onto the table in the breakfast nook. By the end of the first week the table was covered, so he took a little extra time to sort through some of it, throw away some of the junk. He popped open a beer and a serpent of foam snaked out and onto the counter. He wiped it up. In the low light coming through the window he saw the accumulation of dust stand out next to the area he had wiped, so he put the decorative fruit bowl and the candy tray over by the sink and dusted the rest of the counter. He dusted the fruit and the wrapped candy. He washed and dried their containers and put everything back where it was. He slid the newspaper from its plastic sleeve. The weather service had predicted rain and whenever they did that, the paper-route people would put the paper into a plastic bag that leaked. Fortunately it hadn't rained. He leafed through the paper.

She called every other day to say hello, but always at work so he would not feel she was checking up on him. So he would feel his freedom. He had been vague about his evenings, a little standoffish, self-protective.

He lingered a little longer each time at her house. Each time he felt a little more comfortable there, he'd read a little more of the paper, even started doing the crossword there instead of waiting until he got home. He'd get a laugh out of something one of the columnists had written and wonder if he should save it, share it with Helen when she got home. One night when he'd finished the crossword, with only one across and one down left unsolved (that was good for him), he stood by the table and fished the 1964 silver dollar from his pocket. He walked into the living room. He wanted to put it back in the desk, but the desk was gone. Maybe the desk is in the garage or something, he thought.

When he walked through the connecting door from the house to the garage, a mass of cobwebs clung to his face. "Shit," he said in disgust as he wiped them away. It took him several tries to get one strand that trailed down his right cheek. As he looked through the garage he kept waving his hand back and forth in front of his face, in hopes of knocking away any stray cobwebs before they launched another successful attack. The desk wasn't there. He still felt foolish about the coin, unable to fathom why he'd slipped it into his pocket in the first place. He thought about where else to leave it, but he couldn't think of anyplace.

*

Quitman was bored with the prattle of his new partner, an eighteen-year-old from one of the suburbs who babbled constantly about his high school conquests on and off the baseball diamond. He used phrases Quitman hardly understood. He ended each and every story with, "And, Dude, I was all." "All what?" Quitman would ask. And the kid would reply, "Come on, Dude. You know. I was like, *All.*" Quitman became able to block out the words, but the voice vibrated in his skull.

He spotted her before his new partner did—who was busy telling him some story about cheerleaders, the school bus, and blow-jobs—so Quitman called her. Calling her gave him priority on first shot at selling her something.

"Coming past the Benz, down on the corner," he called, pushing out his chair and heading toward the door.

The woman, with blonde-streaked hair, coming onto the lot from the corner, was packed into tight faded jeans that were stuffed down into calf-high boots and a snug white sweater that was cinched at the waist with a broad purple belt. She didn't look side-to-side to inspect the cars. There was something about her. The way she carried her clutch purse tucked under one arm, holding the end of it with her hand.

"Helen. Jesus," he murmured as he burst through the double doors and onto the lot. She waved at him. He hurried to her. "How are you? You look great. What happened to your hair?"

"Nothing happened to it. I got it done. You like it?"

He beamed a broad smile. "When did you get back?"

"Last night. But I decided to surprise you."

"It worked," he said. He felt like he'd been poked on

the shoulder in passing. Just enough to push him off-balance. Her walk was snappier, her carriage more erect, the light from her eyes was kicked on high. Then, his eyes drifting down her sweater front, "They new, too?"

"You're not mad, are you? They're just bigger is all. I don't know, I just wanted to. Don't be mad. They feel so real," she said taking his hand, "feel them." She placed his hand on her breast, but he snapped it quickly away, blushing for the first time in his recent memory.

"Not here."

She touched her index finger to his chest, "But you'll feel them later, won't you? Please say you're not mad."

"I'm not mad, but. . . . "

"Don't say 'but.' "

"Why the change?"

"I don't know," she purred, coyly drawing an arc on the ground with the toe of her new shoe, "I just wanted to." Her body stiffened, rigid with determination. Her green eyes fixed on him. "You only live once."

"No kidding?"

She turned a quarter-turn away, leaving him to occupy only the corner of her sight. "I'm serious, Quitman O'Neil. Don't make fun of me."

He felt the nape of his neck tingle like a scolded child's. "I'm not. I'm not making fun, just surprised." He moved to be in front of her again.

"I want you to like it. But even if you don't like it, I do." Her shoulders relaxed and the boot toe went back to its invisible artwork. "Say you're not mad. It's my first day back. I haven't seen you in over two weeks. Tell me you're glad to see me. Did you miss me? Are you sorry I came to see you? Do you want me to leave? Have I been a bad girl?"

His ego swelled with the belief that she had done what she had done for him. Then his mind muddled with a confusion of jealousy and fear, lust and inadequacy. He watched the nipples of her new breasts push against the sweater and he watched the play of the sun in the ash-blonde streaks in her hair. The breeze carried the burnt scent of the peroxide past his nose. "I missed you."

"Come over tonight?"

"Please." Quitman said.

"Can I kiss you?"

"Then all my customers will expect it."

She made a pucker of her brick-red lips and for a second Quitman wasn't sure that they weren't new, too. She blew a kiss at him. "Take that, my baby. See you later."

"I read something in the paper last night that was funny. I'll show it to you tonight," he said.

When Quitman reentered the building Jerry, the manager with the bald head, standing inside the door in sea-green patent-leather loafers and sport jacket to match, said, "Who's the old broad?"

"Fuck you, Jerry," Quitman said.

Back in his cubicle, Quitman thumbed haphazardly through Marty's metal card file, drawing out cards at random and reading them: Bill Springer. Wife: Joy. Children: 2 girls—Alegra and Felicity. Sports: Football, Vikings. Baseball, Cubs. Drives: 88 Toyota. Wants: Family car, 4 door, wagon. Trade: no. Work: Engineer. Credit: A1. Phone: . . . .

Quitman smiled at the next card, "Jesus, Marty, you kept these cards at home?" he chuckled. "Carmen Esparza," with nothing else filled in but the phone number; scrawled across the bottom, "Thighs like butter. Just touch them and they spread." "Did you try to sell her a car, too, Marty?" Quitman flipped Carmen's card at the wastebasket like a playing card at an inverted hat. The

first name on the next card stuck in his throat "Bob . . ."
He stared at the card, his eyes barely seeing it. The card
felt cold to his touch. It fell from his fingers and did two
flips on the way to the floor where it landed, face up, to
stare at him. "That son of a bitch could be in here."
Suddenly it was new again; the dark, sweet odor of the
earth piled at the foot of the grave. The dryness of his
cheeks in the hot, white sun. The vision of Marty in the
trunk of that Lincoln—it all rushed through the valves of
his heart. Flutter. He looked away from the fallen card
and reached for the phone.

"This is Fresh."

"Fresh, this is O'Neil. I've got Marty's card file."

"What?"

"Martinez. Marty. I've got his client and lead file. All
the people he'd done business with."

"Where did you find it?"

"His wife gave it to me. The day of the funeral."

"Why didn't you say something?"

"I don't know. Never thought of it. It just dawned on
me, now. He could be in here Fresh, the guy who killed
Marty could be in here," Quitman picked the card from
the floor, slid it into the box and shut the lid. He spun his
chair to face away from the file, away from the killer,
away from the sudden rushing back of Marty's brutal
death.

"Can you bring it to me?" Fresh asked. Getting
no reply he continued, "O'Neil, are you still there?
O'Neil?"

Quitman snapped back, his eyes regaining focus,
"Yeah, yeah, I'm here."

"At work?"

"At work."

"Stay there. I'll come get the file."

Fresh stuck his head into Stevenson's office on his way out. "On the Martinez thing—" His face erupted into a bright smile when he saw her sitting there. "Maria, hi," he said.

She sprang lightly from her seat and hugged him. "It's nice to see you," and then, as though once wasn't enough, "it is. It's really nice to see you."

"I wish I could stay longer bu—"

Stevenson interrupted, irritably. "What about Martinez?"

Fresh continued, "O'Neil found his client file."

"Good," Stevenson said, flashing his caps, "this could be quite a break for us."

"We could have lunch, maybe?" she asked Fresh from the sidelines.

"I'd love that."

"So would I."

"Something to go on anyhow," Fresh said to Chief Stevenson.

Stevenson moved so as to block visual contact between his daughter and Fresh. "Keep me apprised."

Jackson Fresh bobbed his head to the side to get a final glimpse of Maria and say, "I'll call you. Or call me."

She nodded her assent and Fresh turned to leave, mumbling to himself, " 'Apprised,' who is this guy?"

She resumed her chair. Stevenson remained standing for a moment, following Fresh's exit with hooded eyes.

"Anyway, Daddy," she began, hoping to snap him out of his fixation on Fresh, "I was thinking maybe Marquette instead of staying so close to home. Don't you think that would be good?"

"So far?" he said, sitting again with the desk between

them. "What does your mother think? Have you spoken to her?"

"Yes. I know what Mom thinks. I wanted to ask you."

"Well I thought this was already decided. Isn't it?"

She looked down at her hands, the nails trimmed neat with only small precise ribbons of white along their edges. She felt like a puppy on a long training lead. Not always mindful of the leash's end; coming up short. Did he want her close or didn't he? Would he reach out to her or not? Would he forgive her? "I don't know, I guess it is, I guess it's decided. I was just having second thoughts this week, I don't know why." She stood and looked at him until their eyes met. Maybe shock would help. "I'm ovulating. Maybe that's it. My thinking always gets a little funny around this time."

He looked away so quickly that for a time his eyes found nothing else to settle on. "Well," he said, placing both hands flat on his desktop, "if it's settled then."

She stood, her toes slightly pigeoned, her hands clasped before her. "Well, I won't keep you any longer. I know you're busy. I feel as though I'm interrupting."

"No, pumpkin," he began, "you're not interrupting, you never are." He then fell silent, offering no new direction for the conversation to go.

She kissed his smooth cheek then wiped away the lipstick trace as he had trained her to do. "I've got to be going. Really."

As she left the building the question she had come to have answered still gnawed at her as it had gnawed before; grinding her like corn to meal. Where had the idea of Marquette even come from, she wondered? It was true, she had gone there originally, as a freshman, but the thought of going back there hadn't even entered her head before she walked into his office and found herself suddenly unable to ask what she had come to ask. Having Fresh come in at just that moment was a stroke of luck. It brought some light into the room and in that light she could at least begin to speak, but about school? What was so difficult about asking, "Daddy, do you love me?"

*

Quitman stood on the showroom floor facing the floor-to-ceiling window watching the lot-boy hose down the cars. The mist from the spray hung like a shiver in the cool failing light. Soon the lights would buzz on and bathe the surroundings with a greenish cast. But now, the cars all faced into the setting sun, their shadows stretched long, fat, and lazy across the asphalt. The sight brought a feeling of calm to Quitman.

"O'Neil."

Quitman focused on the glass and Fresh's reflection in it. Without turning he said, "It's on my desk. Third cube, you remember?"

"I remember."

When Fresh's retreating reflection had shrunk to the size of his fist, he turned and followed him. "Will it help?" he asked, stopping in the doorway.

"It could. I don't know. It's the best thing we've got so far, I can tell you that for sure."

"So you've got nothing yet?"

"Nothing. Nothing to go on, nothing to get."

"Do you people take classes in this stuff?"

"What stuff, dammit?"

" 'Nothing to go on, nothing to get'—where do you get that crap?"

"You still don't get it, do you? It's not my job to discuss my job with civilians. We need to know what you know, not to fill you in on what we know. We don't have time for that."

"Make time."

"I'll tell you this. We've got no fingerprints, no reliable description: You couldn't pick him out of any of the books you went through, nobody witnessed it. All we got is he's about your size, maybe a little bigger, about your build, maybe a little huskier, brown eyes but you're not sure, brown hair but it was probably a wig. That narrows it down to an adult male maybe from this area. That gives us a little less than three hundred thousand alibis to check. That could take some time, you agree?" Fresh read the distress in Quitman's eyes, "I wish we could do more, really."

"Me, too. Is there anything I can do? To help I mean?"

"Maybe you can help me eliminate the least likely."

Quitman slid the other chair up to the small table. "How do we do it?"

"Remove the professionals and those with excellent credit." Quitman shot a puzzled look at Fresh. "In instances like this, it's usually more profitable to work from the bottom up."

"People with good credit don't kill?"

"Sure they do. They're just less likely to brutalize, that's all, so we save them for last."

"Well, Jesus, it could have been anybody."

Jackson looked at him intently, "Now you know how I feel."

"Remove the women?"

"No. Could have been a boyfriend. Use the same criteria for them. Can we work here?"

"Sure."

Three hours later the smoke from Fresh's cigarettes hung above them like a thunderhead in the tiny cubicle.

Quitman's eyes burned in the dense air; he rubbed them with the heels of his hands.

"Bothering you? You want me to quit smoking in here?" Fresh offered.

"It's burning but that's okay. I promised myself when I quit I wouldn't become another pain-in-the-ass reformed smoker. Let's just get out of here for a minute, go down the hall for a coffee or something."

"Doughnuts," Fresh said appreciatively when he eyed the remains of the two-dozen assorted, "they're good to you here."

"Good, shit. I bring those in."

"Why?"

"It's a long story. It just pays to have friends in a business like this."

"I see."

"Are we making any progress? You take cream?" Quitman asked as he drew two coffees from the large silver urn. He reached the bottom of the pot. The black muck released an acrid smell that was almost visible. The small, laminated counter was sprinkled with a gritty coat of spilled sugar that stuck to the side of his hand. He brushed it away. Looking around he added, "I hope not, cause we're out."

"Black's fine. Yeah, we're down to twenty possibles. Like I said, at least it's something to go on, someplace to start."

*

"This is VanDyk."

"I've been waiting for your call," Lyman said, sitting straighter in his chair, "It's been three weeks."

"Denver was a bust. Records that old are kept in a central file. Some of the data's been converted to computer, but not this stuff."

"Where are you, now?" Lyman demanded, shifting his weight forward on his elbows.

"Like I said, Denver wasn't the place to start, Washington was, so that's where I am. I may have found something, or at least an approach. A couple a dozen middle-level bureaucrats retired in 1964. And a few of those had something to do directly with the physical minting of coins. What d'you think?"

"Very possible. A good possibility," Lyman sipped his brandy and relaxed back into his chair, letting his bulk slacken, allowing his eyes to nearly close. "What will you do next, Mr. VanDyk?"

"Back to Denver."

❧

VanDyk's hotel room overlooked bold stands of pine and capped, defiant bursts of mountain but all he said to the woman in the room with him was, "Doesn't it ever fucking do anything in Denver but snow?"

She looked at him over the top of her half-frames, her brows thick and laced with gray above her yellowed eyes. She pulled the dangling Camel from her lips. "Sometimes," she wheezed, and coughed against the back of her hand, "sometimes."

VanDyk waved away a veil of cigarette smoke in front of his face. "What did this guy, this Meyers, do at the Mint?"

"Quality control. Final inspection and weight. He worked upstairs from me."

"Did you know him?"

"Not in the biblical sense," she said, smiling at her own wit.

VanDyk was bored. Five days of interviews had failed to turn a shred of anything useful. Insurance investigator, what a laugh. Trying to find an heir. The older the trick the better, he thought. Days of eliminating the other names. Days at the newspaper. Days on the telephone. "Just how well did you know him?"

"I was at his funeral."

VanDyk felt his heart push up and try to vomit from his mouth. It's got to be him, he thought.

"And his wedding," she concluded.

He swallowed his heart. "Who did he marry, do you happen to know?"

"Helen Costello."

"You've been very helpful to our company, Mrs. Courtland. If you'll just fill out this form, my company will send you the payment we discussed." Like hell, he thought.

It took a day and a half. Eight hours on Tuesday, four hours on Wednesday, but there it was, the marriage license. James Gregory Meyers and Helen Louise Costello.

Back in his room, VanDyk called every Meyers in Denver and asked for Helen. Strange, he thought, how a common name like that could be so unpopular. Good thing though. It helps to not find any.

At the library he used his pocketknife to remove the Ms from his home-city directory. He called all the Meyers there. Nothing.

At the Department of Health he learned that Meyers had died of complications involving the kidneys, liver, and stomach. What they call in Ireland, "The Drink," he thought.

Back at the newspaper morgue, he almost banged his own stupid head against the fucking wall when he came across the obituary: "Survived by his loving wife, Helen Costello." She kept her own name. The bitch kept her own stupid name.

This time his penknife cut out the Cs.

It didn't take long. Even a meandering river rushes when it reaches the delta.

*

Quitman sat on the floor and shifted his buttocks until he was comfortable. He leaned his back against the sofa. Helen pulled a cushion from the couch and sat next to him.

"Want a fire?" she asked, gesturing toward the fireplace.

He looked at her. He disliked the idea that her new breasts kept stealing his gaze from her face.

"Do you like them?" she asked.

"What?"

"You know," she said, drawing back her shoulders, presenting her chest. "The things you can't keep your eyes off of. Do you?"

"I'm sorry. My mind's somewhere else. I was thinking about Marty. I feel so stupid. I've had that card file thing of his for over a month."

"You just didn't think it was important."

"I just didn't think."

"You're not a policeman, Quitman. Stop punishing yourself, it won't do any good."

He sipped at his drink. The sweet bourbon warmed his lips.

"Is it okay? Need more ice? More soda?"

"No. It's fine, it's great. Maybe Fresh can get somewhere, now. Maybe I'll get some sleep at night."

"I know," she began, rubbing her finger lightly across his neck, "even when you sleep through the night, you're restless."

"Do I keep you up?"

"Sometimes, but I don't mind."

"I would, if I were you."

81

"But you're not, so don't worry about it." Her lips brushed his cheek. "Mommy doesn't mind, honest."

"I just hope Fresh gets the bastard."

"He seems like he's trying, at least from what you've said."

"I think he is. I just don't know how well *try* and *do* come together in his profession. You know what I mean?"

"I think so." Seeing his glass near empty, she reached over and tentatively placed her fingers over his, "Want another?"

"Let me make you one," he said as he rose and stretched in an effort to work a kink out of his back. "What are you having?"

"Just some wine. The open bottle's in the fridge."

Quitman poured her wine and made himself a drink. Standing there, at the sink in the kitchen, he tried to look out the window into the dark night, but all he saw was his image reflected in the pane. It was not the face he expected to see. The cheeks and eyes were calm, more than they had been in several weeks. He smiled at himself and suddenly was aware that he hadn't smiled much lately. Not a real smile, filled with joy or hope or abandon; a business smile, now and then, perhaps, but not a smile that felt good all the way to his groin and brought with it a flowing sense of relief. The onus of Marty's death left his shoulders. From his back to Fresh's. In the wink of an eye. In the flash of his smile.

"What's taking so long? You okay?"

He turned and shot her a smile that erased any anxiety in her mind.

She smiled back. "What's up?"

"Nothing. I mean, I just feel like I've done my part, understand?" Quitman said.

"Not completely."

"The file, Marty's file. I feel like I've done what I can, you know? What I'm capable of. The rest is up to them."

"I'm happy for you, Quitman."

She approached him. He opened his arms, a glass in each hand. She pressed herself against his chest. He enjoyed the firmness of her breasts against the bottom of his ribcage. "Are they sore?"

"What? Wait," she laughed, "don't tell me we're continuing the conversation I tried to start a half-hour ago. Are we?" she said, not lifting her ear from his chest, savoring the resonance that vibrated through her when he spoke. "Is that it?"

"That's it. Are they sore?"

"A little from the skin stretching, but mostly in my belly button where the incision is."

"Belly button?"

"That's how they do it, now. Have you decided? Do you like them?"

"I don't know," he teased, "can I see them?"

"Oh, you bet," she purred.

She stepped back a little, took her wine glass from his hand. He set down his drink. She leaned against the counter, reached back and dialed the light rheostat to low. He opened the buttons on her blouse as she sipped at her wine, the fruity bouquet filling her nose. He opened the front panels of her blouse, revealing her chest.

The breasts were larger, but other than that looked the same. He took one into the cup of his hand and it felt as warm and supple as picked peaches that had sat in the sun. He kissed the nipple, took it between his teeth. . . .

"Gently darling," she asked. Her free hand ran through his thick hair, flat-fingered going forward, nails down coming back.

The hardened nipples dipped spoutlike at the ends.

Her fingers splayed on the back of his head. She pressed his face closer. She assisted by pushing upward as he lifted her to sit her on the counter. She leaned her shoulders against the cabinets, her head lulled forward, her eyes rolled shut.

Between kisses he said, "They feel real to me."

She replied without opening her eyes. "To me, too."

☙

From the bed Quitman asked, "So what did you do today?"

"What?" she asked from the bathroom.

"I asked what you did today—anything?"

"I went shopping, that's about all. I was at the mall for almost four and a half hours."

"What'd you get?"

"Nothing. Just looked," she said, walking into the bedroom.

"Four and a half hours and you didn't buy anything?"

"That's why they call it shopping, silly. If you brought something every time, they'd call it buying. It's fun. You ought to come with me sometime."

"Oh. Sounds great."

"Don't be sarcastic with me."

"I'm not."

"I can tell from your voice you are." She sat on the bed next to him. "Your voice and the way you roll your eyes up." Her hand on his cheek guided his face around toward hers. "What's the matter, don't you think we could enjoy each other's company in a mall?"

"I don't like to shop."

"There are places to eat there, places to get a drink. Besides," she rose and walked around the room shutting off the lights, "how will I know what to get you for Christmas if I don't ever get to see you looking at things?"

"Christmas is a long way off, Costello."

She stood facing the highboy and struck a match to light the hurricane lamp. She considered her face in the oblong mirror, cast in orange by the flickering flame. She gazed deeper into the glass at Quitman's image. "I'll still know you then, won't I?"

His eyes met hers in the reflection. The question hadn't occurred to him. He hadn't thought about Christmas—or more precisely, Helen and Christmas. A sudden hand grasped his heart. Yes, he thought. Of course . . . God I hope so . . . "Probably," he answered.

She turned toward him, unbuttoning her shirt as she advanced. The silk slid from her shoulders. She stood before him. "You don't mind if I sleep without a shirt, do you?" She slid into bed.

"Let's go to a movie tomorrow, what do you think?"

"I think that would be fun," Helen said, nuzzling her head into the crook of his shoulder. "What should we see?"

"Doesn't matter. You got something in mind?"

"No."

"I don't go to work till three. Meet me at the Royal Ten a little before noon, we'll just pick one there."

"Can't we go together?"

"Got to go in the morning. Make sure my evening

deliveries are prepped. Nothing's more of a pain than not having a car ready for a customer. I'll meet you there. See a show. Have some lunch." Her gentle hug flushed warm blood to his flesh and suddenly he was drowsy and content.

Nine

Maria felt light and centered after her workout. It cleared her mind. The sheer monotony of exercising had a way of sweeping away the cobwebs, straining whatever enzyme it was that caused anxiety out of the blood. She was always amused when one exercise guru or another tried to credit the enormous boredom of exercise to some zenlike state, but then, it could just be that feelings of higher consciousness and ego-surrender were nothing more than boredom after all.

Jack Fresh had called, as he had promised, and they were meeting for lunch at the Bristol. She'd known him since she'd known anything; he was among her earliest memories, a fixture at the birthday parties and Christmas eves of her childhood.

The sun was low and cool in the fall sky. The gentle breeze caused the dry eucalyptus leaves to rattle like the shuffling rice inside maracas. Usually she wouldn't have walked the two or so miles from the gym to the Bristol because of all the unwanted attention a pedestrian, and especially a woman, gets in Southern California. But the day was exactly the right weave of cool sun and warm breeze, of slight haze to take the edge off the light, of blood flowing easy and even through her system, and she just couldn't resist. As she walked she filled with the freedom of it. She felt restrained only by her own inner sense of purpose, her own desire to go the direction she was going. When the sidewalk ran out she took to the hard-packed dirt with easy strides and headed out to cut diagonally through Memorial Park.

The Bristol sat at the north end of the park with its back facing the frontage road they shared. Under the limbs of the aged willows she could see the weathered lattice that walled in the patio of the café. Along the path she was walking the dense trees kept much of the grass in shadow most of the day so it remained damp and held the rotting aroma of moss close to itself. As she got closer the rich, sweet scent of the white-wine sauce dominated the atmosphere and she responded by swallowing a gulp of the delicious air.

She caught sight of him through the crisscross hatches of the lattice. He looked expectant, his body poised on the edge of his chair in the foyer. His face seemed passive, defined by the full lips, ready to brood or pout, perhaps even to smile but at present uncommitted, open.

When they spotted each other she saw his elastic mouth stretch into a broad smile to match her own. She waved as she anxiously crossed the space between them where they fell into a friendly embrace.

"Jack, it's so good to see you," she said. Better even, she realized, than the other day when her father had seemed to be standing between them.

His hands remained on her shoulders as he moved his head from side-to-side examining her as though she were some rare treasure he held in his grasp. "How have you been? You look great."

There, in the still, cool air of the enclosed patio she felt flushed. Her skin glazed with a light coat of sweat. She wiped at her brow with the back of her fingers and said, "I walked over, it felt great," and she fluttered her blouse front to move the air that was lying against her flesh. "I hope I'm not late. At least not too late. I hate it when other people are late, don't you?"

"I just got here myself." Turning toward the hostess in the flared, black skirt and fringed, white peasant blouse he continued, "Two. In the corner's fine," and he and Maria followed the ample hips as the woman moved through the room.

He poured his Bud into a glass, something he liked to do but seldom found convenient. "It's been a long time."

Yes, it had been a long time, she thought. She also thought it peculiar, as she sat across from someone she truly loved, that she had practically lost him from her mind. She hadn't thought of him in months, maybe even a year, or more. Then, when she saw him the other day, all of her feeling for him surfaced as though it had never been shuffled away to wherever the mind sends things when they're stored in its all-but-forgotten category. "I like this place. Glad you thought of it. Do you come here much?"

"No, but I pass it on the way home."

"You mean when you get to go home."

"Something like that," he began, shifting his weight in his chair, relaxing against its ladder-back. "But I was home last night. ESPN had the gymnast's semifinals from Argentina. The Polish girl that won; she had nothing on you."

She blushed a slight pink color into her cheeks. He was the only person who knew her from before the accident that didn't seem to feel embarrassed for her, and who was not afraid to mention gymnastics. "I didn't see it but the talk around the gym this morning was that it was a lackluster event at best."

"I wouldn't have thought of *lackluster* to describe it but it fits it perfect."

She sipped thoughtfully at her goblet of Eye of the Swan. "Ever since the accident everybody has treated my athletic experience like it's something I'm trying to forget, something I should be trying to put behind me. My father's the worst. As far as he's concerned it never happened. I never trained day and night. We never sat together and dreamed; planned. It was everything and now he pretends it was nothing. Even now, even, what is it, a dozen years later? I'm glad I have you, you're the only one I can talk about it with . . . I don't regret a second of it," she added, though the welled tears at the bottoms of her eyes implied it was not completely true.

"Why should you?" After a pause he continued. "You know, I'd have thought he'd be over it by now. I guess I thought I knew your Dad better than I actually do."

"I don't think anyone knows him, he's changed so much, or maybe it's that he hasn't changed at all. Maybe he locked up back then and can't get started again. Sometimes I feel sorry for him. Can you believe that?"

"I can believe it," he said, lighting a cigarette.

The gray-blue smoke drifted like a lazy cloud in the still air. The acrid scent stung when she breathed.

It's the faces that you grow up with that frame your understanding, she thought, as she looked across at him. There it was, one of the most important faces in her life. The face that took the place of her father's face after the accident. The face that was there for her. The face that filled her adolescent fantasies. The face on the man against whom she judged all other men. She reached over and touched his large hand. She was relaxed and comfortable in his company and it resonated in her tone,

"What about you? I mean now that we've covered the past, and me, what about your life, Jack, how are you?"

He took a long drag on his cigarette, seeming to inhale the smoke all the way down to his toes, before grinding it out in the ashtray. "I'm the same as I was a dozen years ago, too." He waved off her scoffing look with a smile of his own and continued. "No. It's true, in a lot of ways I am. I still hate California but I can't bear to leave. The weather's so damn monotonous and the days so similar it drives me crazy. Half the time I have to concentrate to know which month it is."

"What about friends, anyone special?"

"Not really. Still mostly too busy. This job doesn't accommodate the kind of compromise a regular relationship requires. Know what I mean?"

"Don't you mean that it deserves?" she said, but she was just playing and they both knew it. She did know what he meant. And while she saw his recognition of these facts in his expression she was less able to pinpoint his resignation to them. A restlessness still lingered in his posture. A hopeful, romantic jitter animated his hands when he thought or talked of love and her witnessing of it caused a bittersweet wave to wash over her. She felt the joy of it more than the pain. She felt more a sense of privilege at being present than the guilt of voyeurism as though intruding—after all, she loved him, didn't she? She thought but couldn't say, "someone will come along." How could she when no one had, in all his adult life, "come along," at least as far as she knew. "Has there ever been anyone, Jack?"

Uncharacteristically, he tried to skirt the issue. "Dozens. You've met a lot of them."

"You know what I mean. Someone more than just for fun."

"What's wrong with fun?"

"Nothing. Not even with the kind of fun you're having with me right now."

He paused. His face grew calm. "If I answer can we let it go at that?" he said.

"Of course."

"Once there was, but you know how that goes."

"That's not fair, Jackson Fresh!"

"You promised, Maria, right?"

"I did, didn't I?"

The afternoon rolled on. Time escaped both of them as though it didn't matter, and at the moment it didn't. Nothing was more important to either of them than each other's company. In each other's presence each of them felt less an obligation to self-preservation. They felt that whatever part of themselves might be exposed to danger their companion would protect. Their guards were down and their relaxation was joyful.

The waiter cleared the plates. The lunch crowd thinned. The hostess rested her generous hips against the counter where the coffeemaker sat. A few waiters and waitresses gathered around her, gossiping and making out final checks for their remaining tables. One gossip group pegged Maria and Fresh as May-December, the other clique had them as father-daughter. Both agreed that it couldn't be hooker and John. After all, what self-respecting prostitute would wear Nikes on a call?

A breeze stirred the leaves and, catching a wisp of the mint fragrance of the eucalyptus, Maria felt she understood what attracted the Koala to them.

In the parking lot Fresh asked, taking hold of her elbow, "Want a ride to your car? Back over to the club?"

At this time of year the sun cut an arc through the sky

more like a line-drive than a pop-up, and the warmth it provided vanished with even the slightest provocation. If it ducked behind a cloud it got suddenly chilly, when it popped back out you could feel its presence. The wind had picked up a little and the sun peek-a-booed through the wisps of cloud. She rubbed her arms as a quick chill gripped her. "Yes," she said, "I'd like that."

"I have something I have to tell you," he said, as the car rolled down the street.

A drop of fear mixed with her calm as she looked over at him. Why hadn't he mentioned it at lunch? she wondered. This is how life's worst comes to light, isn't it? *I have something I have to tell you.* "What is it?" she asked.

"It's not monumental or anything, L'il Brat," he began, using his pet name for her, "It's just official. You can take that worried look off your face. I just didn't bring it up at lunch because I was enjoying myself too much, that's all."

Smiling, rotating toward him as much as the seat belt allowed, "Well what is it then?"

"Your friend, Quitman O'Neil."

"Quitman, what about him?"

"He's a suspect in one of my cases."

"What kind of case?"

"Murder."

"Quitman? I don't see that as possible. He's not the type."

"Come on, there is no 'type.' You and I both know that."

"Oh you know what I mean, Jack. He's too much 'Live And Let Live' for that. He'd really have to be backed in a corner for that and even then I'm not so sure that that would inspire him to kill someone."

"Do you still see him?"

"Does my father know?" she asked as it dawned on her that she was involved in this investigation by her association with Quitman.

"No."

"Thank you for that."

"I still might keep an eye on him from time to time. I know it's none of my business if you see him or not but as other people become involved in the investigation, other officers, you know, your knowing him will come out. It'll be impossible to avoid." The spot in the parking lot next to her Fiero was available so Fresh rolled the brown four-door in next to it. He unsnapped his seat belt and turned toward her. "So?"

"So, I haven't seen him in a while, that's so. Any other questions, Detective?"

He moaned, put his hand across his eyes and rubbed. "Don't be that way."

She scooted over the vinyl seat and kissed his cheek. "I'm sorry, really I am. I appreciate what you've done. My father would appreciate it, too, if he knew." Then she said, "I love you," and squeezed his hand, scooted back across the seat and got out of the car.

Ten

VanDyk saw the steam from the shower building in the open bathroom doorway as he silently slid open the closet door. Many of the new clothes Helen had bought still had the tags dangling from them. On an upper shelf, alongside a pile of sweaters, he found a clutch of framed coin sets. He walked over and sat on the bed. When he heard the water stop he stepped into the bathroom.

She threw back the shower curtain. She didn't notice him at first through the thick steam—her eyes still blurry with water. Then her bowels clenched like a fist. She screamed. His right shoulder dropped and the force of his weight drove the fist that lifted her from her feet and slammed her to the floor. She was dazed near the point of unconsciousness. She was helpless to stop him as he dragged her by the hair across the tile and over the carpet to the bed. Her eyes tried to focus. "Please."

He pulled his knit shirt over his head, kicked out of his loafers, undid his belt, and stepped out of his pants.

Her eyes widened in horror. She struggled to sit up. He grabbed her hair, lifted her, struck her hard at the arch of her ribcage. He let her drop back, gasping for breath. His weight threatened to suffocate her. She was thankful that she was only half-aware, lapsing in and out of consciousness—hungry for oxygen.

When she tried to cover herself he jerked the blankets from her. He threw the framed coin set on the bed. The glass in them shattered and scattered over the mattress and her vulnerable flesh. "Where are the rest of them?"

She sobbed. She knew the truth, that there was no rest-of-them. She wished there were more. "There are no more. What do you want? Please leave me alone."

He used a pocket knife to cut two strips from the sheets. Desperate, she tried to squirm away. The broken glass dug into her palms and knees. The side of his fist pounded the small of her back. She writhed in pain on the glass, cutting herself in a dozen more places, blood coming from each of them.

He worked quickly binding her wrists to the headboard with the strips of sheeting he'd cut. He yanked her face toward him by the chin and slapped her until her blubbering subsided. "Where are the rest?"

A low moan escaped her. A helpless, forlorn, nonhuman wail that broke into convulsive sobs. Her words were jumbled, bubbly with the thick phlegm in her throat, unintelligible.

He slapped her again. He held the open blade of his knife before her eyes.

She held her lower lip clinched, to the point of bleeding, between her teeth. She wanted to look away but something inside her compelled her wide eyes to follow the blade's path.

He laid the cold, silver steel blade along the inside of her arm, two inches above the wrist. He slit the artery. She fainted at the sight of the spewing blood.

When she came to she could hear him in the other room, upsetting drawers and flinging books. She was afraid to look from side-to-side. She felt strangely warm, strangely warm and drowsy.

Quitman wondered all afternoon what happened when Helen didn't show up at the theater. He called and left the name of the movie he was going to see on her recorder. As an added precaution, he slipped his business card under his wiper blade with the same notation on it. Everytime a latecomer popped through the door of the theater, spilling light across him, he thought it would be Helen. He was sure that he'd find a message when he got to the agency but there hadn't been one. He called again, no answer; he left no message. He'd started to turn toward the hallway and the manager's office to see if he could arrange for his deliveries to be handled by someone else—even if it meant losing half the deal, half the money—when the little man said, "Good afternoon, Mr. O'Neil."

Quitman placed him immediately. "Mr. Hackett, isn't it? Look, you'll have to excuse me. I was just leaving." He noticed something new about Hackett, something he hadn't noticed before, an odor that hung around him like the smell of an unattended illness, the aroma of neglect.

Hackett caught his arm as he tried to pass and brought his rotting teeth close to Quitman's ear and rasped in a whisper, "It concerns the dead salesman."

Quitman spun full on him, tearing his arm from his grip. "What about Marty? If you know something, why don't you go to the police?"

"Not so loud, Mr. O'Neil. You're attracting attention."

Quitman looked around the room; other conversations had stopped. He lowered his voice but his anger was still apparent. "What about him?"

Quitman grabbed Hackett by the elbow and steered him through the outside door.

Hackett's eyes darted around at the people wandering through the lot. "Is there some place we can talk in private?"

"Not here. This place is a fucking fishbowl."

"Come to my shop, then."

"I told you I was just about to leave."

"Now. If you please."

They got in the Porsche. Quitman sped the few miles to Hackett's coin shop. Except for a video store, with no customers, all the other shops in the "L" were closed. Quitman slammed to a screeching halt under the awning in front of the door. He ached to know what the eroding man knew. His throat burned with energy.

Hackett unlocked the door. They made their way to the rear of the shop by the low-level illumination that emanated from under the display cases. "Where shall I begin?"

Quitman glared.

Hackett continued, "When you first entered my shop you inquired about a coin. The 64 D silver dollar. There is a possibility that such a coin exists."

Quitman sunk his left hand into his trouser pocket and clutched just such a possibility. Quitman wondered how he could have missed it. How could he have not noticed the pervasive odor that hung in Hackett's shop? The visible filth that settled everywhere. "Go on."

"I contacted an associate of mine. . . . "

"Who?"

"I don't think names are important."

"But I do, they are to me. Don't play games. Who?"

"Mr. Henry Lyman."

"Never heard of him."

"It isn't surprising. He is a man very much behind the scenes. At any rate I thought to make a business deal with him." Hackett kept pausing to assess his companion. His glassy mouse-eyes checking Quitman's reaction. His speech stumbled from his lips, stilted, almost broken. "For the coin. If it could be located. But he double-crossed me. He sent one of his employees to extract what information I had," gesturing to his dirty sling.

"Who?" Quitman demanded again.

"Lester VanDyk."

"He have brown hair and a beard?"

"Goodness no. He is quite Nordic in appearance."

"Six-two or so, very well-built?"

"Yes, but blond and clean-shaven."

"Did he kill Marty?"

Hackett paused. He looked over the top of his spectacles, still trying desperately to judge Quitman's probable reaction. "Of course I have no way of knowing for certain, but yes, I'm sure he did."

"Jesus! Why?"

"Mr. O'Neil, calm yourself. I don't think they meant to kill him. He thought it was you."

"They wanted to kill me?" Quitman screamed. "The fuck would they want to kill me?"

Hackett cringed. He put his good arm across his chest, holding his guts in place. "They just wanted the coin."

"What the hell's so great about this coin that they'd kill a guy for it? And why would they think Marty had it, Hackett?"

"From the only clue I had from you when VanDyk questioned me." He paused to rub his slung arm. "Your license plate number."

Quitman paced agitatedly. "So poor dumb Marty's dead because he borrowed my demo." He spun toward Hackett. "And because of you."

Hackett held his one good arm extended before him as he backed away. "No. Wait. Mr. O'Neil, please understand. I had no intention of any such action. They doublecrossed me. I swear."

Quitman stopped and studied Hackett. "So now you want to doublecross them? Get them out of the deal? How do I know you won't send this VanDyk after me?"

"He is no associate of mine. You must believe me."

"Why is this goddamned coin so valuable? I still don't get it."

"It is *so* valuable because it doesn't exist . . . or isn't supposed to."

"What?"

"They were all to have been melted down before they were ever released. To certain collectors that coin would be invaluable."

Quitman leaned toward Hackett, trying not to breathe through his nose. "What's it worth?"

"To the right buyer, almost anything."

☙

Quitman called into the dark house, "Helen, you here?" He flipped on the kitchen light and walked toward the living room, "Hey, Costello. where—"

He froze. A lump formed in his throat, making him gasp for breath. His eyes darted around the room, from the books torn from the bookcases to the slashed sofa cushions and inverted drawers, their contents scattered across the floor.

"Helen," he yelled, clutched by desperation. Zigzagging through the debris, he sped toward the bedroom. She was naked on the bed, lashed to the headboard by a sheet around her chest, her arms strung out, like the crucified Christ, tied to the posts. Her deep crimson blood stained the sheets, no longer running from the slits in her wrists, it spattered her body at a hundred points where the broken glass had punctured her ivory skin. Her fingers were already turning blue. Her eyelids lulled three-quarters closed, giving her face the look of a child fighting sleep and losing. Blank. Pitiful.

He slumped to the floor, his back banged against the door frame. "Helen," he moaned.

He couldn't have said how long he sat there, perhaps an hour, maybe more, trying to screw up enough courage to look at her again, to get up and cover her with something. His hands lay limp in his lap, his face hung dumb with shock. He kept trying to swallow the lump in his throat. He felt his heart beat at the surface of his skin, in his shoulders, at the base of his spine. Time and meaning were activities happening only in other places. Life was different here, in this hallway, where death slammed a sudden door. Things here existed only as shadow or echo. Even the light seemed a phenomenon with less vibrance and agility.

He cut the bonds and her arms fell, lifeless; thump, thump into the ivory-white blood-spattered lap. He draped the blue and white comforter over her body.

"Jackson Fresh, please . . . O'Neil. Oh fuck. It's *O-N-E-I-L* . . . O'Neil, that's right."

❦

"Being a friend of yours is dangerous."

"You don't have to worry, Fresh," Quitman said. They stood on the walk in front of Helen's house, refreshed by the cool evening breeze as a stream of uniformed and plainclothes police flowed up and down the walk, in and out of the house.

"What'd you know?"

The bittersweet blossoms of the blooming trees drifted by him on a sudden rush of air. It didn't seem right, he thought. "Nothing. Absolutely nothing."

"When you got here, the house was like that? She was like that?"

"Except for her arms. She was fucking strapped up like the fucking Christ. I cut them down," he shuddered as the memory slapped him.

"You shouldn't have done that."

"Arrest me."

"I might."

"For what?"

"Tampering with evidence."

"Give me a break, Fresh—I couldn't look at her like that."

"Gruesome stuff. It could have taken her three, maybe four hours to die."

Quitman didn't realize how hard he gnawed at his lip until he tasted the blood. What do you think about when you're dying an inch, a minute at a time? What do you feel? That it's all going to be alright? That it's not as bad as it seems? "Spare me the details, okay? Just spare me the details."

"You really are a suspect in this one."

"That's bullshit."

"Who else? Did she have another boyfriend?"

"Not that I know of. What are you getting at?"

"Just asking questions."

"Why not try coming up with some answers? The fuck would I kill her for? The fuck would I tear the house up for? The fuck anything. Can you tell me that?" Quitman strode up and down in front of Fresh, flailing his arms, talking rapidly. "I don't know what it is about you, Fresh. Do you piss everybody off?"

"Calm down, O'Neil. Tell me, when was the last time you saw her alive?"

Quitman felt a violent flutter, a stone passing through

his heart. "Alive, my God," he said, looking over Fresh's head into the distance. "Alive. You know, Fresh, we wander around like death doesn't exist, then suddenly there's a person you'll never see again; you wish you'd have looked at them more. Just sat and looked at them. No matter how much you did it wasn't e . . . fucking . . . nough. You know those dots you chase on your eyelids? The harder you chase them the more they're just not there? Fuck my life. . . . It was this morning. I saw her alive this morning."

"Did you spend the night?"

"I spent the night. What next, huh? You want to know what we did?"

"Not particularly."

"She sucked my brains out and I fell asleep in her arms. You can go home and beat off in the shower to that."

"There's quite a difference in your ages."

"Tastes vary. When it comes to certain things—age, race, height, eye color—none of that shit matters."

"Certain things like what?"

"You done with me?"

"Things like what?"

"Love's one." Quitman turned away.

Fresh looked at his profile cast in silhouette by the setting sun, aflame in the red-orange light. "You loved her?"

Quitman waited for the silence to settle in. "You done with me?"

Fresh shook his head in weary frustration. He tucked his shirt and hiked up his pants. "You'll have to keep yourself available."

"Is that the modern way to say 'don't leave town?'"

"Pretty much."

Quitman started down the walk then stopped and

turned back. "You fucking guys, you know." He waved his arm at the police parade passing them on the sidewalk. "I can't figure out what it is you do. Are you really just a bunch of perverse Western Union messengers delivering singing telegrams of death? Are you really from the Department of Sanitation? Stuffing bodies into zippered trash bags and cleaning up the mess? You sure as fuck don't find the people who make the bodies you cart away."

"You're upset so I'm going to let that pass like you never said it. But you're on thin ice, O'Neil."

After a moment he said, "Do you know someone named Lyman?"

"No, why?"

"How about VanDyk? Lester VanDyk?"

"I've heard of him. Why?"

"What about a scrawny guy named Hackett?"

"Never heard of him. What's this about?"

"Marty. It was VanDyk. VanDyk killed him."

"How in hell do you know that?"

"Hackett told me VanDyk did it, on orders from Lyman." Quitman's ribs shrunk tight around his lungs. His next breath could convict him, if not of murder, at least of stupidity, of petty, stupid theft.

"Answer me. How do you know that? Why would this Hackett tell you something like that? How do you know him?"

"He was shopping for a car. He brought up the subject of the dead salesman and told me he knew who did it."

"And he just told you that? In between questions about the car? What are you trying to feed me, O'Neil?"

"I'm just telling you what he said, that's all." Quitman kept backing up, casually, as though what he was telling Fresh was just a thought in passing.

"There's more to it. What aren't you telling me?"

"Nothing."

"I think you're lying. Why would someone just come up and tell you that?"

"What am I, a mind reader? How would I know?"

"And what about you?"

Quitman lunged toward him, his face so close that Fresh could feel the heat of his breath, "What about me?"

"How do you fit into this?"

"I don't," Quitman said, turning from Fresh and walking toward the curb again, "I don't fit in."

Eleven

Except for the light that oozed around the blinds, the apartment lay in darkness. Still, even in the gray-black light, Quitman's personal spirits paraded before him. Marty, dressed sharp as a tack, with every blue-black hair vaselined in place, quick, switchblade smile, his olive skin scrubbed clean. Mom and dad, their drinks in hand, their laughter, their battles, the moaning nights, the brittle mornings, the shell of their love hovering over him like a cracked ceiling. And Helen, now characterized in his mind with enormous melon breasts, her frail arms outstretched with the blood running from her wrists and dripping from her elbows. Running forward to embrace him. Like a veteran without any legs whose toes begin to itch, Quitman felt her hands on his back and he jumped. He shook his head. Kneaded the bridge of his nose. Flipped on the light. Put his hand to his chest and inventoried his pounding heart.

An hour later the phone rang.

"Haven't heard from you in a while. You're a celebrity."

"Maria, hi."

"You sound out of breath."

"No. I was just sitting here. Must have been almost asleep or something." He stretched himself, extending the phone an arms length away so her voice came from a distance. He hardly heard what she said next.

"I even heard your name around the house. My father mentioned it," the cop's daughter added.

" . . . Does he know we know each other?"

"No. Jack deleted it from the reports."

"Jack?" he said, unfamiliar for a second with his first name. "You mean Fresh? Why would he do that?"

"We've been friends for years. Jack and my father used to be close, but even after that changed we remained friends. If my father ever finds out that he fooled with the reports, there'll be hell to pay; but Jack's always taken care of this 'little brat.' " She intoned it the rushed way Fresh would when he spoke it. "Dad's worried enough about me without knowing who spends the night—or at least, who used to spend the night," she said without shyness.

Quitman ignored the implication. Still, he liked hearing her voice. Something in his cortex loosened, a warm relaxation washed over him. "I need your help."

"For what?"

"Can I see you?"

"Not at my house. Not at yours either."

"Why?"

"They're watching you."

Invisible fingernails scratched his spine. "Again? Why?"

"Check into a motel or something," she said, ignoring his question. "Will you?"

Silence.

"O'Neil? Will you?"

"How do I get rid of whoever's following me?"

"You're clever, you'll think of something. Call me when it's safe. Okay?"

"Yes."

"I'll wait."

He yanked a leather duffel from the closet shelf and a pile of folded sweaters cascaded to the floor. He slid them aside with his foot and packed the bag with enough clothes for several days.

He swung the Porsche into the agency lot and up in front of the lot-boy. "Mattie," he said, getting out of the car and leaving it running, "you got time to get this thing cleaned and detailed for the line tomorrow?"

"You changing demos?"

"Going back to my own. It's out back." He waved his hand vaguely in the bright warm air. "Can you hose it down for me?" Every time Quitman sold a car he'd tip Mattie for his prep work; favors were no problem.

"I'll get it out for you."

Quitman tossed the keys to Mattie's upheld hand. "Thanks. Clean it up in back, okay?"

Mattie shrugged, "In back? Okay. You're the boss."

"Come in here, O'Neil," Jerry commanded from his office door when he saw Quitman entering the building. "What the hell happened to you yesterday? Three deliveries and you're off somewhere fucking around. I got half a mind to take you off the deals completely, how would you like that? No money. Nothing. You don't want this job just say so."

"I don't want the job, Jerry."

"What? What is this, O'Neil, some kind of Iranian fuck-stick?" He leaned across the desk, glaring. "Well even if it is, I got the end of the stick that don't have no shit on it, you get it?"

"I don't want your fucking job. Make up my final check."

"Turn in your demo."

"Just did."

"How many miles you put on that thing? You hot shits think you're invaluable. Another hundred people just got off the bus, asshole."

"Drop dead, will you?"

"In your dreams. Get out of my office."

"What about my check?"

"Next Monday."

"Today."

"At close of business."

"In twenty minutes."

Jerry's eyes burned hot at Quitman. He hated to lose him. He was good, a little too temperamental, took things a little personally, but all the good ones did. Did some low-life, son-a-bitchen manager hire him away from me? he wondered. "In twenty minutes."

"Thanks."

"Get out of my office. Didn't I already tell you that?"

Quitman sat his duffel on the Formica washstand in the restroom. He pulled a paper grocery bag out of it and transferred his clothes to the sack. He stuffed the duffel with dozens of hand towels yanked quickly from the dispenser. He placed the paper bag behind the planter at the front door as he went out. He pulled the keys from the Porsche's ignition. The trunk popped open with a metallic clunk. He unzipped the duffel and pretended to painstakingly examine its contents before placing the bag inside. He gently lowered the trunk cover, locking it in place. It had been easy to spot the car following him, once he knew enough to look for it. The plain-Jane four-door with blackwall tires.

Back inside, he retrieved the paper bag and strode down the corridor.

"Here's your check."

"See you, Jerry."

"See you, kid."

He found his own car clean and ready to go out back. "I gassed it for you," Mattie said.

"Jerry'll love you for that." Quitman pressed a twenty into the lot-boy's palm.

"You going for good?"

"For good. . . . So long."

❦

Quitman eased the Lincoln down the ramp and into the hotel's underground garage.

"I need a single for a week."

The clerk rotated the registration back toward himself. "Yes, Mr. Inge. Your luggage?"

"In the car. I'll get it myself, later."

"It's four twenty-five. To the left of the elevator."

The Kelly green bedspread had a knobby surface. That theme carried over to all the textiles in the room. The television was tucked demurely in the corner. The security bolts that kept the guests from stealing the pictures off the walls were well concealed. The lighting was indirect. He carried the phone to the window and slid open the curtain while he waited for room service to answer. The room overlooked an inner courtyard fifty feet below. "This is four twenty-five. Send up a fruit and cheese tray, a bottle of Dewars, ice, and soda."

"Right away, Sir." The phone voice tried for an add-on sale but Quitman wasn't buying.

❦

"Maria?"

"Where are you?"

"Downtown. The Tower. Four twenty-five."

"Be there soon. Do we need anything?"

"If we do, they'll have it here."

The cheddar cheese was beginning to sweat by the time Maria's knock came on the door. She reached up to kiss his cheek in passing as she marched into the room. "I knew it," she said, "that's the fourth pair of panty hose this week." She sat on the edge of the chair to examine the run at the back of her calf, then spied the bottle of Dewars. "Oh, you're a doll. Make me a Scotch. I'm sorry it took so long but, I got to thinking, Jack left me out of the report but that doesn't mean he's forgotten we know each other. Anyway, I drove around for about an hour to make sure I wasn't being followed. I don't think they would, but I wanted to be sure. It's better to be safe, don't you think? Don't you think runs are ugly? Doesn't this look ugly to you?" she asked, turning in the chair so that he could see her calf.

Quitman waited, wanting to be sure she was done. He handed her a Scotch. "Thanks for coming. It's good to see you."

"It's good to see you, too, it's been awhile," she said, taking clear nail polish from her purse and applying it to the tear in her hose. "So, tell me, how do you rate so much attention from my father and his band of merry men?"

"I know some people who died."

"More than one? Both murdered?"

"Murdered!"

"Did you do it?" she asked, looking up at him. "Hey. Don't look at me that way. We don't know each other all that well, but I don't think you did it, I trust you or I wouldn't even be here. So I'm just asking."

"No, I didn't do it. I just knew them is all."

"I believe you. I know what it is to be under suspicion. For my whole life I've felt like I was under investigation. You should have a cop for a father sometime. So what's it all about?"

"You won't believe it."

"Try me." She stepped out of her shoes and slipped behind the high-backed chair to wiggle out of her panty hose. "You don't mind if I take these off, do you? They're just so ugly. There," she said, stepping back into her heels, her calves tightening upward, presenting them to him for inspection, "that looks okay, don't you think? I mean, this outfit isn't so dressy that it really needs hose, is it?"

Quitman mixed himself a Scotch, long on soda. He wasn't sure where to begin or how much to tell. The blood in his hands and feet ran icy, generating a chill dew in his palms. He stopped by her chair, facing the window. Maria's face was an object on the periphery of his vision until she touched his hand. Suddenly, there on the edge of his eye's awareness, she became Helen. He jerked his hand back.

"I'm sorry. What's wrong?"

He moved around in front of her, gaining the coffee table between them; Helen vanished and Maria's firm coiled body sat before him.

"You alright, O'Neil?"

He answered, "Yes," without conviction.

"Talking might help," she probed, easing herself back into the chair.

With the silver dollar held in the arch of his index finger, Quitman lowered his fist to the table's surface and a flick of his thumb sent the coin whirling like a top. It crept along in an ellipse until it ran out of energy and rattled down to rest. "That's it."

"That's what?"

"What it's all about. Why we're sitting here drinking Scotch. Why I'm dinner conversation at your father's house. Why the cops are following me. Why two people are dead."

"A silver dollar? Don't you want to tell me? It's alright if you don't, but maybe I can help."

Quitman had to tell someone and although he felt an intimate trust for Maria at that moment, she could have been anyone, even Fresh. Once he began, the story spilled out of him with the usual awkwardness of truth.

*

His body was crammed into what felt like a cabinet. His knees jammed against his chest, the ceiling so low that his head bent forward, his chin touching his knees. The rear wall chafed like brick against his back, but the rest smelled like wood. A small diamond of light fell across his left eye from a crack in the front wall. Horrified by what lay before him on the bleached plain, he struggled to look away but could not. Dozens of people lay scattered in disarray, in shock verging on coma, just beyond hope. Among them skulked panthers, visible breath grumbling in their throats. The low-lying harsh light flung their broad shadows over the earth, their steps raised billows of dust from the dry, brittle ground. He heard moaning when one would pause to toy with a near-lifeless form, see a flurry of sudden activity, a batting of paws, a glint of switchblade claws in the terrible light. A cat looked toward him. Its head swung low between its shoulders, a pendulum moving in measured ticks. Its sullen eyes froze on his. It lumbered toward him, the massive scapula on its back undulating its silken fur. He fought to look away again but could not. The beast's gaunt head bobbed before the tiny opening, causing the light to kaleidoscope in Quitman's eye. The hot, vulgar breath splashed over his face. The smell of rotting meat filled his cell. The beast was haunched on its hind legs, its paws battered the wood: bangbangbangbang, bangbangbangbang. Quitman pushed with all his might to straighten himself and woke to find himself falling to the Kelly green floor.

Bangbangbangbang. The room door. Maria's voice, "Are you alright, O'Neil?" She rushed from the bathroom. "Is that the coffee," she called through the closed door. "Can you leave it in the hall; I'll leave a tip when you pick it up." A clatter of the cups as the tray touched the hallway floor. "Are you okay?" she asked Quitman.

"Bad dream. I shouldn't have slept in the chair." He started to rise, then groaned, rotating his shoulders, then his head. "I wasn't made for this." He looked at her. Even though she was wearing the same clothes as yesterday, she looked fresh, although he bet she didn't think so.

"Bad dreams are more than where you sleep. Honest, you've got to stop blaming yourself. So you dropped the coin in your pocket, so what?"

"None of this would have happened if I hadn't done that, that's what."

Maria stood at the mirror ironing her clothes with the palms of her hands. "Be realistic, O'Neil. I mean, really. Look at it like this. Did this woman. . . . "

"Helen," he interrupted.

"Did Helen like you? I mean, do you think she cared about you?"

"Yes."

"Even that first night? I mean, you weren't just a roll in the hay for her, she wasn't like that, was she?"

"No, she wasn't."

"Well, then look at it this way. What if, when you'd found the dollar, you'd have told her how much you liked it, what then? God, these clothes look tacky. Do you think they look tacky? Tell me the truth. Hmm? I'll tell you what, then. She'd've said 'why don't you keep it,' just like any other woman in the world. Women will give men anything, anything they've got. Don't you know anything about us, O'Neil? Oh God, I can't stand it. I'm going down to the lobby to get something to wear." She took his face in her hands, "Stop blaming yourself. I'll be right back." Before he cared to say anything, she was gone.

Standing at the window, he looked down at the inner courtyard four floors below. He saw Maria's taut body as she strode out of the elevator corridor and across the carpeted and tiled lobby. She walked without regard to the architect's intent, ignoring the neatly laid paths, opting instead for the straight line.

What she had said made sense, but what was the value of sense? It wasn't Quitman's gray matter that ached, it was his heart. It wasn't logic he longed for, it was love.

"Forgive me," he said to Maria the moment she returned.

"I do." She held a bag of new clothes in both arms. "Now, forgive yourself, not that you have anything to be forgiven for."

"I wish I could believe that."

"You'd better. You didn't take advantage of anyone, you didn't abuse anyone, and you didn't kill anyone. Two people you cared a lot about are dead."

A chill radiated from his heart. "I know they're dead," he said defensively.

"Doesn't that make you the least bit angry?"

Her words cracked against his mind like a baseball bat. His senses sprang alive. He tasted the anguish and smelled the crimson lacquer of Helen's blood, felt the blue-coldness of her fingertips. The bright knife blade fought his tears for space in his vision. He was more alive than he wanted to be.

She laid the bundle on the chair. She walked around behind him, slid her strong arms around his chest, and held him fast.

"Let's get them," she whispered.

Twelve

---

aria's Fiero charged along the snaky canyon road,
surefooted as a cheetah beading down on its prey.
She handled the car with grace. Downshift for the low
outside curves, accelerate for the high banks, flat-out the
straightaways just for the thrill of it. The gear box
hummed, the cabin vibration massaged them in their
seats.

Quitman strained to hear her over the roar of the
wind through the opened car windows. "What?"

"I said, don't you think it's a good idea to visit a couple of coin dealers, just to find out what we're dealing
with?"

"Can we roll up the windows?"

"What?"

Quitman reached across to the center console and
drove the windows shut with two small levers. "Can you
hear me now?"

"Yes. I'm sorry. I just like the windows open. Especially when the oleanders are in bloom like now. Can
you smell them? Bittersweet?"

He'd picked up the distant smell of cow dung, but he
had no idea what an oleander looked like, let alone what
one smelled like. "What were you saying?"

"We'll stop at some coin shops, try to get an idea of

what the coin's worth. Did you know that oleanders are poisonous? When they're burning, you can die from the fumes."

"I'll avoid smoking the leaves. Coin shops will just tell you the coin doesn't exist," Quitman said, and he was right . . . at least at the first two dealers. The first one told them that coins are minted all the time that are just melted down; somebody's always starting rumors about valuable issues that don't exist. The second one just said, "There's no such thing. Unless you've seen it, of course."

When Maria braked the car to a stop in front of the third dealer, she twisted the rearview mirror around and studied her face. She swashed on fresh lipstick with a broad brush, then asked, "Would you be upset if I did the talking this time?"

"No."

"How do I look? Okay? How's my make-up, do you like it?"

"Looks fine. You look great."

"You're sweet." Her dark lashes fluttered slightly.

Her thighs strained at the hem of her short skirt as she extricated herself from the car. Quitman followed her into the shop.

The glass in the cases sparkled flawlessly. It was set at angles with the lights to avoid reflections. Nondescript music played just loud enough to muffle the drone of the air conditioning.

"Good afternoon. How may I serve you?" The young clerk stood with his hands joined before him, well back from the counter. Must be a style with these guys, Quitman thought. Unlike Hackett's shop, with its wrought-iron entry gate and fenced-in walls, this shop was bright and airy, with large detailed lithographs of coins and engraving tools on the beige walls. The light came from sconces along the wall and from hidden lights above the decorative headboard. He thought he caught the scent of lilac but when he sought it it was gone. Quitman didn't feel like an intruder here, more like someone with a special pass.

"I might as well tell you right away, we don't know anything about coins. By the way, I'm Maria Stevenson," she said jutting her open hand toward the clerk. He shook it limply as she continued. "And this is my husband, John." The clerk did not extend his hand to Quitman nor did Quitman extend his own, they simply nodded. "We've been married three months."

"How nice," the clerk replied.

"I'm pregnant. Can you tell?" she asked, presenting her profile to the clerk, drawing her hand down her stomach. The clerk shook his head politely. "You can't, can you? You see, honey," she tossed aside to Quitman, then back to the clerk, "six months and no one can even tell. I'm on this terrible diet, and the exercises . . . John's mother told me all about when she had him, it was real different then, what with the drugs and being sedated during the delivery and all, but now they kind of put you in charge of your own body, which is good, don't you think?" She drew a bead on the clerk. "We've been together since college," she said, giving Quitman a tiny hug, "but we just thought, with the baby on the way and all, that we should get married. Have everybody in the family have the same name. I mean, I took John's name, none of that hyphenated stuff, just took his and dropped mine. It was an awful name anyhow, 'Krakenhauser.' German. Awful to pronounce I mean, of course, not really awful like, well, you know. How would you like a name like that? Would you wish you could get married and change it?" She paused long enough to giggle, then went on, while the clerk obviously wished he could change the station. "Anyhow, we thought it was time we started planning for our baby's future. We thought about stocks and bonds and t-bills and all, but that sounded so boring, don't you think? I mean if you're going to invest in something, it should be fun, something the whole family can share. Couldn't you just see us sitting around the den at night, reading the fine print on our stock certificates to a little child? I mean really, that sounds silly, doesn't it? So we thought we'd find out about coins."

"Perhaps you'd be more interested in precious metals, something with an intrinsic value that can't help but improve over the long run," the clerk suggested, stifling a yawn.

"Ugh," Maria opined, crunching up her face. "What would the baby do with those? Use them for building blocks? What do one of those things weigh anyhow? What if one of those bars of bullion fell on its little foot?"

Quitman coughed to hide his sniggering. Maria turned to him, "It's not funny, John. Sometimes I wonder what's happened to your sensitivity since we got married." She turned back to the dumbfounded clerk. "Coins are meaningful. They have a real meaning in the real world. They're historically significant, and they're beautiful, don't you think?"

"That's very well put, Mrs. Stevenson."

"Please, just call me Stevie. I like my new name so much, I ask everybody to call me that, even my mother."

Quitman was seized with a fit of laughter that he successfully disguised as coughing, "Is there someplace I can get some water?"

"In the rear, Sir, there's a water cooler."

Quitman meandered among the glass cases. Even coins rated as "fine" or "very fine" appeared badly worn to him. Better than used cars. No maintenance, no fix up, no warranty. Dreams for sale, he thought.

"Wise collecting takes much study," he heard the clerk conclude as he returned to Maria's side.

"What's the main reason coins increase in value?" Quitman asked.

"As I was just explaining to Stevie, it's basically scarcity and condition," the clerk said.

"Oh, John, I've learned so many things. Peter," she said, smiling at the clerk, "would you mind telling John what you just told me, you know, about the illegal coins?"

"Not at all. You see, in the earlier history of American coinage, many mint employees, especially executives, saw their jobs as an open avenue to private gain. Some even went so far as to mint nonexistent coins, save them for a number of years, then offer them for sale. Two of the best-known of this type are the 1913 Liberty Head Nickel and the 1804 Silver Dollar. Coins such as these are very rare and practically untouched by human hands, so to speak."

"At another shop we were in, Peter—we've been shopping around a little, you should be proud that your prices compare well—anyway, at this other place the owner mentioned a 1964 Silver Dollar."

"Yes, the peace dollar."

"Skeptical?" Quitman asked.

"Personally I am, yes."

"Why?"

"For one thing, security is better in the minting process now, and for another, the time span. No illegal coin has ever taken this long to surface. What would the holder be up to? Greed and patience just don't go hand-in-hand. It's a fable that collectors enjoy speculating about over a few drinks to romanticize their passion. But if a single coin did escape, not for its value but just as a keepsake, it either has, or soon will, disappear with its owner. In either case, it doesn't exist, or might as well not, you see my point."

"I do, Peter. Don't you, John?" She glanced at her watch. "Oh God, look at the time, I still want to look at baby furniture today. Even though I still have three months, mother said I may not feel like shopping, or doing much of anything for that matter, the last two months. I don't think so," she said, pausing and turning her face to look directly up into the clerk's eyes, "but you never know, do you Peter?"

*

The Rein and Lantern sat tucked in a corner of the hotel lobby, its booths covered with canopies like old two-seater wagons. The inside glowed from the light of candles hung on the wall in cut-glass cases. The waitress slid the drinks in front of them, "Two Scotch and sodas. Will you be dining with us tonight?"

"Just the drinks, right Stevie?"

"Right."

"You're something."

She smiled, sipped her drink, used the napkin to tidy up the already clean table, and dabbed her lips. "I just wanted to put him at ease."

"It worked. If you hadn't been a pregnant married lady he'd have followed you home like a puppy."

She leaned forward, her sinewy arms on the table. The cool, oak tabletop refreshed her skin. "What next?"

"I need to think," Quitman answered.

His thoughts flickered like a candle blown by a breeze not quite strong enough to extinguish it.

He could hear the muted clatter of dishes, the hushed

striding of the waitresses across the lush carpet. It relaxed him to feel the presence of people working around him without intrusion and the first sips of his drink flowed languidly through his veins. "The funeral was a joke."

"Pardon me?"

"Both of them, really. Both funerals, Helen's and Marty's. The priests not even knowing their names, what a joke."

"Did they go to church?"

"Marty did. Parishes are so big, who's a priest supposed to know? The only other funeral I was ever at was for my parents. I was too busy crying to notice much else. Even Marty's kid Gloria didn't cry."

"How old were you?"

"Sixteen. Pretty stupid."

"What?"

"Bawling like that at sixteen."

"It's alright for a man to cry at any age."

"I've heard that, but somehow always from women, never from a man. At least not one I respect."

"That's silly."

"No, it's not. It's like me telling you, when you're unhappy, to bottle it up. Women generally cry, men generally don't, it's that simple."

"Probably why men die sooner."

"Probably. Still, it was a joke."

"Speaking of jokes, I heard one this morning when I went to buy clothes. Want to hear it?"

"I'm trying to talk to you and you want to tell me a joke?"

Maria leaned back against the booth and lowered her eyes, looking momentarily like a lost child in a cathedral, forlorn. "I don't know what else to do," she said, clearing her throat.

They sat silent for several moments, then Quitman said, "You don't know what to do and I don't know what to say; this is great." He reached out and, after a moment's hesitation, she took his waiting hand. "Heard any good jokes lately?"

With injured voice, "Don't make fun of me."

"I'm not. Maybe a good joke's just what we both need. Is it dirty?"

"No, Quitman, it's not," she said, taking back her hand and sliding the napkin from under her drink, dabbing at her eyes, her nose. She dug in her purse and produced a tiny mirror that she frowned into. "I look awful. Do my eyes look puffy to you?" With a small puff, she worked make-up along the lower lids of her eyes. "Can I use your napkin, please?" she asked, as she painted her lips. She folded the napkin and blotted her lipstick. "Any better?" she asked, looking up at him.

"Much," he replied. Why fight it?

"Thanks. This farmer was walking down the street with a three-legged pig and another person came up to him and said, 'Pardon me but I noticed that your pig only has three legs.' "

Quitman looked down at the table where her lips were abstracted on the napkin, sensuous and inviting, staring up at him.

"Are you listening?"

"Sure."

"Did you hear the part about the other man asking about the three-legged pig?"

"What three-legged pig?"

"You weren't listening."

"Start again."

"Maybe," she teased.

"Come on, Stevie," he said, smiling.

Standing in his hotel room, with the windows facing inward to the atrium, Quitman watched the couples gather at the gates of the two restaurants. As the crowd grew, their sounds drifted up to him like the laughter of a far-off flight of geese. The elegant women pirouetted as they moved like fine porcelain dancers on a music box. He wondered why it was customary for women to wear their hair swept up in the evening, their necks pale and exposed. He wanted to kiss each one, exactly where the first bone of her spine visibly pressed against the skin. He wanted to kiss Helen's neck there, lightly, just a brush of the lips. Feel the tiny, nearly invisible blonde hairs tickle his lips. Hear her suck in a breath, giggle. He watched until the courtyard emptied itself into the restaurants.

"I don't know what I want. That's part of the problem, I just don't know what I want."

Maria sat with her legs tucked under her in a captain's chair next to a small table in the corner of the room. She sipped her drink. "Between what and what, O'Neil?"

"It flashes through my mind. The money. It makes me feel guilty."

"Minds explore possibilities. That's what they're for."

"You'll fit right in at college in the fall."

"Who told you I was going to college?"

"Fresh."

"That rumor was started to appease my father more than anything else. Besides, it's true."

"What, that you're going to college in the fall?"

"No. That minds explore possibilities."

"Very intellectual but very unsatisfying. I'm wrestling

with an emotional problem here. Two of my friends are dead and I shouldn't be considering profiting from it."

"You have a way of putting things together in your mind that's, I don't know, frustrating to me," she said, drinking.

"To you? How do you think I feel?"

"You're not guilty of their deaths, you're not even responsible. Quitman, you're not even involved, except as a friend. Maybe what you really wish is that you never knew them. Explore that possibility."

"Your intellectuality pisses me off. You want another drink?" he asked, pouring some of the Dewars into his own glass.

"And that's another thing, aside from your swearing. Just what does *pisses me off* mean? It's not even very visual. I can't even imagine it. *Angry* I can at least see, even *infuriate*, but *piss me off* means nothing. Yes, I would like another drink. You're not facing an emotional problem here, you're facing a tactical one. Does that make any sense?"

"Yes, it does." The Scotch gurgled from the bottle into her glass. He dropped in a few ice cubes, poured in some soda. "There's not a chance in hell they're ever going to catch anybody, is there?"

"The chances aren't good."

"How often do they solve murders when they have nothing to go on?"

"You mean no motive . . . ? Not often. Seldom."

Silence settled between them. His pulse was visible at his temples, regular and strong. He sipped his drink and then began to speak with a precision she hadn't heard from him before. "Tomorrow, Stevie, I want you to go to a motel, one of the chains, one with a pool. Rent a pair of rooms, one on each end of the pool and call me with the room numbers. Get uppers if you can, okay?"

"Uppers?"

"Upstairs rooms."

Her eyes sparkled in the light. Her lips hung open like the abstraction on the napkin, "You're growing up, O'-Neil. I like it."

Maria called Sissy, a friend from work, and confessed, "No I don't really have the flu. I hope you won't tell anyone, but I needed some days off and I'm out of vacation time. Some friends are in town, Bill and Judy, you remember Judy from high school. You don't? Well, she was a few years ahead of us; anyway, Judy's cousin Phil is with them, what a hunk. Sissy, I've had a crush on this guy since we were kids, since before I can remember, even. Anyway, I was thinking of renting a car when I remembered that you had a four-door. I could never get four people in my tiny car. Honestly, I need to save some money. Do you know what it costs to rent a car? It's ridiculous, I hope you never have to. I couldn't believe it. Would you swap with me for a couple of days? You would? Oh Sissy, I don't know how to thank you. If it works out between Phil and me, just think, I'll owe it all to you. Tell them at work that you talked to me and I sounded terrible, that I just need quiet so I can rest? I'll be back in a couple of days. I really don't know how to thank you. Oh I hope I can, I do, I hope I can do as much for you someday. You don't know what this means to me, really, Sissy, you're a princess. Can I come over now and swap with you?"

Good. Quitman was pleased. She wouldn't be driving around town in a car that every member of the police force recognized on sight, and she wouldn't be in a car with rental plates.

Thirteen

Well, I really can't tell you how," Fresh began, "cause I don't know. He went to work, took a bag in with him, that made Patterson suspicious, so he kept going from the front to the back, trying to cover both exists. Then O'Neil came out the front and put his bag back in the car so Patterson settled down and watched the Porsche. When he didn't see O'Neil coming out to meet customers, he went in to look for him. He was gone, drove away in his own car. Quit and drove away."

Folding his hands before him, Stevenson asked, "Did he get a description of the car?"

"Yeah, but there's another hitch. It's not registered in this state and no one there ever bothered to notice which state it was registered in. The lot-boy said the plate's background was white, maybe greenish. The lettering was either blue or green according to him, but I felt that he likes O'Neil and was lying because he thought it might help him in some way, out of some kind of perverse loyalty. One of the other salesmen said the lettering was brown or purple on gray. I've faxed his vita to the states with some combination of those colors. We should be hearing something soon."

Stevenson swiveled slightly in his chair, his fingers pursed at his lips. This wasn't good in his eyes. This case was a loser from the start. A man and a woman murdered, by a stranger, for no apparent reason. How much more hopeless did a case have to be before you washed your hands of it? He wanted to turn this case out to the general pool, to "Networking," from the start. Get it out of his area, off of his statistical count, but Fresh wanted a crack at it. He shouldn't have listened. Fresh had caused him trouble in the past with his outdated approach. "I'm turning this project completely in your direction, Jack. Perhaps I've hindered your progress in some way, I don't know. At any rate, your approach seems sound to me. You can maintain the four men you have now and coordinate this in any way you feel is best. Just let me know from time to time what's happening, Jack."

Fresh rose from his chair. "Why this all of a sudden?"

"What do you mean by that? Why *what* all of a sudden?" Stevenson snapped. "I'd've thought you'd have wanted this."

Fresh knew arguing with his superior wouldn't get him anywhere. He mustered his best sarcastic tone, "Thank-you. Is that all?"

Fresh sucked slow even breaths as he walked out to the parking lot. Beyond the lot lay the area where abandoned cars were stored, waiting for auction. He wove through aisles of them, stopping in front of a Plymouth. He laid his hands palms-down on the hood. His breath hissed in and out of his mouth. His hands jerked up violently and plummeted down, buckling the hood. One quick step backward, then his foot flew up, shattering the left headlight. Three steps sideways and the right headlight exploded. He skulked around the car, punching windows and kicking fenders and doors until, finally exasperated, he collapsed against the back fence. "I expected more than this from you, Stevenson." The leather of his shoes bore deep cuts and scrapes but they did not bleed like his hands, they did not throb like the veins at his temples. For all his frustration, all he could say was, "Fuck me."

❦

"Hi."

"Where are you?"

"The Motel 6, off Euclid."

"What room?"

"I'm in two nineteen."

Quitman made a loop from the hotel on his way across town and he spotted the unmarked car parked down the street from his condo. He fought the urge to pull the cop from behind the wheel and find out just what the hell he wanted. He wasn't guilty. He was only friends with dead people. Didn't they intend to do anything about the deaths beside following him?

"Not a bad room for a place at the 6," Quitman said.

"A little small. You can't even walk around in here."

"Motel rooms aren't for walking, Stevie," he said with a smile.

"What do you think, I was born tomorrow, O'Neil?"

"That's good, I like that. *No* is the answer."

"What now?" she asked, sitting on the corner of the bed, kicking off her shoes, and drawing her feet up under her.

He sat next to her, rubbed his face with his palms, then turned his face toward her. "I'm not guilty, but I know who is. The fuck are the cops following me for, can you tell me that? They can't think I did it, that I killed Helen and Marty, can they? It seems so stupid to me, a waste of time. They could be doing other things, maybe even something productive for chrissake."

"They are."

"Are what?"

"They're doing something productive. You really don't get it, do you, O'Neil?"

"Get what?"

She avoided his eyes. "Oh, O'Neil," she began. She jumped up, her fists clenched at her sides as though to keep herself from exploding. "Quitman, they don't think you're guilty. They're not that stupid." She spun toward him, clenched fists at waist level, crouching slightly, her eyes hot. "They think you're next. Can't you see that? They have an idea who did it, too. They just can't prove it. They need them to come after you." Her arms dropped to her sides, limp.

"Is that why you're here?" he spat.

"Go to hell," she yelled, making a clumsy attempt to get back into her shoes, "Just go to hell." . . . Giving up, she bent down and snatched her shoes up, her arm jutted toward him, the shoes pointed at his face. "Just remember, O'Neil, you called me. *Remember?* Do you? Do you remember that? What am I, a witch? Did I put a spell on you to get you to call?" She jerked her purse from the dresser and scurried for the door. He leapt in front of her. "Let me out of here, you bastard."

"Let me talk to you first."

"No. Get out of my way!"

The heel of one shoe caught him just below the eye. He whirled away from her and the flung-open door struck the small of his back, dropping him to his knees. By the time he got to his feet, he could see her storming past the pool, head down, purse and shoes clutched in either hand, her arms rigid at her sides.

He was alone. Not only physically alone. He felt uncomfortably light, as though not even the air of the room touched him. Stranded. Unable to draw a satisfying breath. He felt enisled, isolated in a bubble with a small prick at the apex. It hissed slowly at first. Those around him gradually increasing their orbit, whirling in the growing tornado, then *bang!* sucked out through the vortex. Some of them by choice, some of them by chance, leaving only the void he stood in now, somewhere between the floor and the ceiling, equally distant from the walls, the air lying slightly beyond his gasp. He slumped on the bed.

He pushed himself up and went to the sink. He examined the reddened flesh under his eye. He flinched at the touch of his fingertips. The cold washrag stung at first. Water trickled down his cheek onto his shirt, and radiated across the cotton.

He had thought of his father as cynical, a man who only talked in quips: "Never do anything for anyone that they wouldn't do for themselves," "Take people for what they are, and not for what you wish they were," "Take for granted, bear the loss." He felt the gray blanket of his father's soul shroud him, and the incomprehensiveness of his mortality became clear as pain. *Live and let live.* It was his rule, but only his. If no one else lived by it, it couldn't work. He'd just tried to live his life, be good at what he did, but it wasn't enough. Other people decided things for him. From the time he got up in the morning to whether he lived or died. Now or later, it didn't matter to them. He peered into the mirror and death sprung out and slapped his face. He was a bystander, innocent or not, clutter in the field of vision of people who knew what they wanted at any price. A leaf in the wind.

"Mr. Hackett, this is O'Neil."

"Mr. O'Neil, I have been looking for you. You have left your employment?"

"Do you know the old Motel 6 on Euclid and Barrow?"

"I do."

"I'm ready to talk deal. Meet me there in room two nineteen. If it takes me a while to get there, wait, understand?"

"How long?"

"As long as it takes if you want in on this."

"What time should I arrive?"

"Within the hour. Can you do that?"

"Yes. But if you're not there, how will I get in?"

"The key's in the planter at the end of the breezeway."

Quitman stripped the drapes from the window and the laden dust made him convulse with sneezing. The hot rubber backing was softened to tackiness by the burning sun. It squeaked against itself as he stuffed them under the bed. He dialed his home phone and patched the call-forward into 219 to avoid the switchboard. He wiped down everything he had touched with a towel, then used the towel to open and close the door before moving quickly down the clanky, metal outside stairs.

From the other side of the swimming pool—room 257—he had a clear view into the other room. Hackett was prompt. Quitman watched his nervous fidgeting in the planter's soil for the key, and grinned at the disdain the unwashed Hackett displayed over the dirt on his hands.

Hackett stood, paced the room, checked his watch a dozen times in the first thirty minutes. Two hours later the phone rang. Hackett startled as though the sound was new to him, and stood motionless through the first three rings, then lifted the receiver cautiously to his ear. He did not speak.

"Mr. Hackett, this is O'Neil."

"Mr. O'Neil, where are you? I have been waiting several hours."

"I'm on my way. I wanted to let you know so you wouldn't leave." He sunk the hook, "The coin is in my possession. Wait for me." He hung up quickly.

He eyed his prey, even more nervous than before. Hackett the squirrel, Quitman thought. He watched him darting around the room in jerky bolts, unable to concentrate, wishing for a way to make the time go faster.

Two more hours passed before Quitman was satisfied that Hackett had come alone, that no one was waiting for his return, that no one knew he was here. He hadn't used the phone except to answer it, he'd had no visitors, there had been no one hanging around the pool or the breezeways trying to look overly casual. Quitman strode the length of the causeway and descended the stair under the cover of the building. Once on the ground, he circled the motel in a wide ellipse, observing every car, every movement. He ascended the stairs to 219.

He spied Hackett through the window just as the coin dealer emerged from the bathroom. He could have something in there, a phone, a walkie-talkie. Dammit. Quitman retraced his steps to 257. Now it was his turn to pace nervously. He snatched up the phone. "Hackett, this is O'Neil."

"Is this some kind of a—"

"Open your door."

"What?"

"Open the door to your room."

For the second time Hackett said, "What?"

"Your door. Open it and look over to the other side of the pool."

Hackett opened the door enough to stick his head out.

"All the way open, for chrissake, Mr. Hackett."

The coin dealer swung the door wide and stood in the frame.

Quitman jerked the drapes open in his room, "Can you see me, Mr. Hackett? Across from you, second floor?"

"Yes, but why . . . ? "

"Don't go back inside. Turn around, toss the phone in, shut the door, and come directly here. Do you understand?"

"Yes but. . . . "

"DO it."

He watched Hackett crossing the courtyard, then lifted the receiver and repatched his call-forward to 257.

Quitman hurried Hackett into the room, slammed the door, and snapped the drapes shut.

"Why all these precautions, Mr. O'Neil?"

"The police are following me."

"But why?"

"It's a long story and not an important one right now."

"Do you have the coin?"

"Yes."

A twinkle brightened the deadness in Hackett's eyes. Quitman thought there might be a little life showing in his cheeks as well. "May I see it?"

"Details first. What's it worth, in concrete terms? I've heard 'invaluable' and enough shit like that."

Hackett shifted in the chair, ran his hand over his throat. "I see your point."

"Do you?"

"I think so, yes. Since we last talked, I have made discreet inquiries; if the coin is in the proper condition. . . . "

"It's perfect. Cut the crap. You think I got it out of a slot machine?"

"No. Of course not. I have been in touch with some European buyers, in Holland actually, who could probably be persuaded to pay up to two million."

"Who?"

"I'm sorry Mr. O'Neil, but I am determined to remain part of this. I will not reveal what I know, no matter what you do." He looked greatly relieved when he realized that Quitman intended to do nothing violent.

"What about the man you mentioned before? What about Lyman?"

"I'd rather not do business with him."

"Would he bid for it? Against the European? I'd sooner get his money after what he did, wouldn't you?"

"I see your point, but he is a dangerous and greedy man."

"Aren't we all?" Quitman sneered.

"Before we proceed, may I ask your intentions concerning a fair division of the profit?"

Play it close. Watch the eyes, Quitman thought. "I'll ask you, what do you think is fair?"

"If I could deliver to you a sum approaching two million, it wouldn't seem unfair to expect twenty-five percent for my agency, my skills."

"I'm a salesman myself, Hackett. Twenty-five points is too much to expect on the front side. Don't look puzzled. You know what I'm talking about. My guess is you're not in direct contact with the man in Holland; you're dealing with a broker somewhere, perhaps in Europe, but perhaps not. Wherever he is, he's sitting in the middle of this pie. Your finder's fee from him is—let me guess at two percent." Quitman paused to watch Hackett swallow. "There's also no real way for me to know what the buyer is actually paying. So your back side could be thick. You've got the best seat in the house. You're the only one, so far," he said, leaning over Hackett's riddled frame, "who's aware of exactly what's going on. From where you sit, you can see the front door, the back side, and everything in between, right?"

Hackett swallowed hard, ducking under Quitman's arm out of the chair. "Surely Mr. O'Neil, you wouldn't deny a legitimate businessman his fair share."

"If the fair share is five percent. Then I don't care, and you can run it from there."

"I wish you'd consider ten percent, Mr. O'Neil. Five is practically unheard of."

"I've heard of it." Quitman said. His nerves tingled in his hands close to the bone, invisible to the eye, an urge to action that he suppressed. He had never been a physical man. He had never been in a fight, unless you'd call those silly skirmishes in grade school fights. He always thought there was another solution, another way to settle things. He saw fighters as cowards, lacking in some basic skill, void of a crucial synapse in the brain, but now Quitman felt the drive to fight. Not just with Hackett, the poor, frail, twisted stick of a man before him, but with anyone in his way.

His mood wasn't lost on Hackett, who backed slowly toward the door, distress filling his eyes. "I came here in good faith, on business."

"You want ten percent? Here's how to get it: Sell the coin to Lyman. Otherwise it's five. No ifs, ands, buts or bullshit. If it's somebody's money we're going to get, Lyman's going to be the somebody." He paced as he spoke. Catching a glimpse of himself in the mirror, he quickly looked away, avoiding death's eyes. "Get Lyman on the phone."

"Now?"

"No, Hackett. Fucking tomorrow," he said, glaring. "Of course now."

"It's late, he may not be available."

"We'll call until he is."

Hackett slowly went to the phone and dialed.

"It's rung several times. . . . " His imploring eyes caught Quitman's.

"Let it ring."

"Uh, Mr. Lyman, this is Emile Hackett," he suddenly spoke into the receiver. "It's regarding the coin, the 64 D. I am in a position to discuss price."

Quitman reached into his pocket, pulled out the coin, and flipped it to Hackett, whose jaw fell slightly ajar as he coveted the prize in his hand.

"What? Yes, I'm here. Yes. Oh yes. More than that. The best proof of all. I am holding it in my hand."

♂

Quitman drummed his fingers on the pocket that once again held the coin. Hackett had gone. He sat on the bed. Having patched the motel phone through his own, it was a simple matter, the touch of a key, to redial Henry Lyman.

"Does the 64 D interest you?" he said without preamble.

"Who is this?"

"Shut up and listen."

"Answer my question or I will end this conversation."

"There are others interested; suit yourself, asshole," he said, slamming down the receiver.

He gave the stew a half-hour to simmer.

"What do you think, Lyman, want to listen now?"

Following a brief silence, Lyman replied, "I'm listening."

"The coin was in Helen Costello's house the day VanDyk was there."

"I don't know either of those people."

"Suit your-fucking-self. If you don't know Lester VanDyk, then maybe I'm talking to the wrong Henry Lyman, maybe I'm talking to someone who's not interested in coins. Maybe you don't even know what a 64 D is. Maybe I should go through the phone book. Maybe I've got the wrong number. That it? Wrong number?"

"Who are you?"

"We don't want to do that again, do we? I'll take a simpler approach, so do what you can to follow this: Are you interested in coins? Now it's your turn to say something."

"I collect coins, that's right."

"Do you know someone named VanDyk? Think carefully."

"I have heard the name."

"Progress. How about Helen Costello?"

"Are you implying that the coin is in VanDyk's possession? I know better than that."

"Do you?"

"Yes."

"Don't think he's maybe dancing with another partner? Think about it. Your ass is in the open here. I'm willing to help you watch it."

"For what in return?"

"Not your undying love, I promise you that. Can we stop fucking around here? I know what it's worth in green dollar bills; all I want is a little."

"You are a fool, my anonymous friend. You have given me all I need to know and it hasn't cost me a cent." The line clicked off in Quitman's ear.

"Oh hasn't it?" he said to the empty room.

❦

Every city has them. Salesmen call them "Sleigh Lots" because of their reputation for selling the same cars over and over. They're easy to spot. Out front are giant painted proclamations: "No Credit? No Problem!" "We Finance AnyOne!" "We Buy Cars For CASH!!!" If you drive in, every available body, from manager through lot boy, hovers around your car telling you how nice it is, how well maintained it looks, how they can tell how you took good care of it from how clean the interior is, how they had a guy in there just yesterday who was looking for something just like this. They're sorry, they say, but the appraiser's out right now. They hope you can wait, he should be back any time now. And wait you do. Three hours is the minimum. You drink coffee, smoke cigarettes, page through the battered magazines, pace. Then someone tells you that the appraiser's buying cars down the street and, to speed things up, they'd be glad to take your car to him, they're sorry for the delay, sorry you've waited so long, business is business, it won't be much longer. You wait. Two hours minimum. You thumb the magazines again. You're amazed you've smoked the whole pack already. Your car pulls back on the lot, your hopes rise. The salesman offers you another cup of coffee. He sits across from you and slides the cup over, then he belts you with a figure sixty percent under low book-value, like he's doing you a favor. Your head reels, he can see it in your eyes, he counted on it. He knows you're desperate. Why else would you be there? They've used up your whole day, no time to shop. You sign. Tough shit. They sell your car two hundred per- cent over book, five hundred down, to anyone who can breathe. In sixty days, they repossess it and drag it back in for the next sucker's sleigh ride. Too bad.

Quitman knew he'd take a beating at Bronco Billy's Fine Used Cars before he even rolled his Lincoln over their curb. Five hundred yards down the street, he bought a Buick and asked them to register it in his girlfriend's name; kind of a present, he said. "Maria?" they asked. "Sure," they said; could have been Mary, Mother of God, for all they cared.

Fourteen
----

is expectations are that he will receive two million. I told you that on the phone."

"Where did he get that figure?" Lyman walked around his desk to face Hackett. "What's your percentage?"

Lyman's large froglike face caused Hackett's hand to twitch; at any moment the hideous face might lash out a sticky serpent tongue and suck him into an abyss. He slipped his hand between his crossed legs for control and aligned all the courage he could muster.

"That, Mr. Lyman, is not your concern. If I am able to deliver the money to my client, I will be able to deliver the coin to you, it is that simple." When he was met with no outrage, the trembling left his voice. "I am here only at my client's request. If it were my decision, I would market it elsewhere, but it is not."

"Who is your client, Mr. Hackett, if I may ask?" Lyman relaxed into his chair, the wingbacks set his face in dark relief, his large hands resting in his lap.

"You may ask, but I will not answer. You said you would have the money. My client is expecting to hear from me."

Lyman rose slowly, lumbered to the far side of his desk, and hoisted a large suitcase onto the glass surface.

Hackett started to reach for the clasps, hesitated, wiped his hands on his shirt front, and reached out again. The clasps popped open and he threw back the lid.

"Newspapers!" he shouted, his face struck white with horror. "You expect me to purchase a two million dollar coin with newspapers? This is your opportunity to own the rarest coin in the world, even more scarce and valuable than the New Hampshire pattern piece of 1776, and all you do is attempt to manipulate the situation, and me?" Hackett slammed the lid on the valise, "Perhaps another buyer would better understand the value of my services."

Lyman set an identical second suitcase on the desk. "Perhaps you're right, in a way. I find it irresistible to overlook the potential drama in a situation. Forgive me." He opened the second lid.

Hackett swallowed two rapid gulps, then touched the back of his hand to his mouth to catch the small trickle of greedy saliva that threatened to escape the corner. The money lay stuffed in the case, not confined with bands, a mosaic of wealth.

"You have two choices, Hackett. You can pick up this case," Lyman said, waving his hand over the sea of green dollar bills, "and return with the coin, your five or ten percent tucked away somewhere, and be done with it. Or you can leave with this one." Lyman's broad hand rested on the newspapers. "Return with the coin and leave here a millionaire."

"But without the money, how. . . . "

"I leave that up to you."

❦

Hackett's thoughts were like whirling dust devils. Sitting at his desk, he eased open the bottom drawer and removed an oily rag which concealed a .25 caliber automatic pistol. He removed the gun; a tiny button on the side dropped the shell magazine into his waiting hand. He used the oily rag to remove the excess dust, clicked the magazine back in place and cocked the bolt, racking a shell into the chamber. If he could have a million for buying the coin with last week's news, he could just as easily have two million for the same effort, didn't that make sense? Why do anything for Lyman, or O'Neil for that matter? Why not do something for Emile Hackett for a change? A lifetime of pittances from undergrading coins had left him with no less guilt than this would. He read it in Lyman's slits-for-eyes, his life was worth nothing here: He was a pest, a fly on a lily pad. Europe had more to offer. Only one thing stood in his way.

❦

"Hi, Jack."

Fresh turned and smiled. "Well, Maria. Nice to see you again so soon. Looking for your father?"

"Thought I'd surprise him. Is he around?"

"Somewhere. Want me to page him?"

"No, I'll give him a few minutes. Be okay if I wait in his office?"

"I'm sure it would be." Fresh pushed out from behind his desk. "I hope I told you when we had lunch the other day that I think going back to college is a smart idea."

"I think it'll be fun," she lied. "What are you doing? Still up to your eyeballs in shit?"

Fresh laughed. "I said that to you when you were what, thirteen years old? And you've never let me forget it. Still true though. This work is like a heart attack, no amount of wishing'll make it go away."

They walked together toward her father's office, Fresh's hands clasped behind his back. "Have you seen Mr. O'Neil?" he asked.

"Quitman?"

"How many O'Neils do you know?"

"Just the one. That's enough."

"Have you seen him?"

"Yes. The other night."

"Where?"

"The old Motel 6. He's not there anymore."

"Where is he now?"

She stopped and placed her hand on his arm, to turn him toward her, "I don't know. Can't you take another approach? You're driving him crazy. He's paranoid."

"If you see another way, tell me. I'll be glad to try it. Something's going on out there, I don't know what, but something; he's involved, doesn't matter if he realizes it or not, he's involved. In a way, we're protecting him, if you look at it right."

"I don't think you could get him to believe that."

"Oh well. What can I say? Say good-bye before you leave."

She tiptoed up and pecked his cheek. "Okay, Jack."

Maria entered her father's office and closed the door. She thumbed through the messages and notes on his desk, shuffled the folders in his active file, nothing. At a sound at the door, she moved quickly around the desk. "Hi, Daddy."

"Well hi, pumpkin." A broad smile lit Stevenson's face as a wary spark lit his eye. He took each of her hands in his. "Nice to see you. What brings you down here?"

"Just in the neighborhood. Thought I'd say hello."

❀

If the underworld and gangland were, as Quitman believed in his childhood, actual places you could go, then he had now embarked, slinking around on a level of life he hadn't imagined before. He was acutely aware of the

145

world around him, yet was invisible to their eyes. He had some planning to do. He'd told Hackett he'd call with a meeting place for the exchange but where would be safe? Somewhere secluded, where he could watch the approach? Somewhere crowded, where he could feel the safety of numbers? What would Hackett buy? Anxiety drove his adrenalin through his brain and he was shocked at how slowly the drama around him moved. At first he'd thought his call to Lyman would take Hackett out of the picture, but somehow he had survived. Not only had he survived, but now he had the money. Quitman hadn't counted on that. He knew it was bad planning, but "gangland's" terrain was unfamiliar to him, he had to take it as it came. So finally he settled. He asked Hackett, "You know the mall, the one with the plaza? Around the fountain. Eight o'clock."

☙

The warm evening air surrounded Hackett, holding the sounds and the sense of the night close to his flesh. He sucked several cough drops, but the dry tickle in his throat refused to be soothed. As he walked forward toward the trunk of the car, he checked his pocket again for the pistol; it was still there, just as it had been the twenty times before. He turned the key, the trunk popped open, and he lifted the tongue-shaped lid. He lifted out the case and closed the lid with a tinny clunk. What a world where you can buy two million dollars for a buck, and his brown teeth crept out between his smile.

☙

Quitman shifted nervously from foot to foot, hating himself for picking this place with its lightly splashing water and surging, gurgling pipes; he had to consciously avoid urinating. He spied Hackett working his way through the throng of shoppers with a brown suitcase. Quitman checked around himself for signs of danger; even though he didn't know what to look for, he felt certain he'd know it if he saw it. A community of people sat on the circular lip of the fountain, the sound of their voices harmonizing like the faint jabber of a distant monkey house.

Hackett stood facing O'Neil, the suitcase between his feet. They stared at each other.

"Do you have the money?"

"Of course I have the money. What do you think, I came all this way with a valise full of old newspapers?" Hackett smiled at his own wit. Warm blood filled his hands and feet.

"Let me see it."

"Not so quickly. Do you have the coin, or did you come all this way with empty pockets?"

"I have it."

"I must see that first then."

Quitman brought the coin from his pocket and extended it on open palm. Hackett snatched at the coin as he pulled the gun from his pocket. Quitman grabbed desperately and the coin locked between their palms.

"I have a gun, Mr. O'Neil."

Quitman was amazed at how gigantic the tiny gun looked from his end. He jerked his hand back; the coin dropped to the ground between them. Hackett looked at the coin, spellbound, as it rattled to a stop. Quitman lunged for it just as Hackett extended the gun and fired. The report boomed.

Quitman looked up in time to see the metal fragments of the exploding gun fling Hackett backwards, into the fountain, where he lay face-up and bleeding from a hundred different-sized holes in his head and chest. Quitman snatched up the coin and turned to run.

He ran smack into VanDyk. Even without his disguise Quitman recognized him, his eyes, in a single horrible instant. His legs locked paralytic and he stared.

"Well, well," the hitman said.

For lack of any better thought, Quitman spit in his face. VanDyk recoiled, dropping his guard. Quitman took off running. He started up the staircase and suddenly realized that every time he'd seen a chase in the movies, they always ran up, but it was a loser's plan. He scaled the banister and landed on a shopper, hurling her to the ground and spewing her packages in every direction. He scrambled to his feet and ran toward the exit fifty yards ahead. Running footfalls behind him slapped the marble floor, reverberating in his head. He plunged into a thick group of teenagers in front of a video arcade, losing himself in their midst.

"What in the fuck is your problem, dude?" one pimple face demanded.

"Someone's chasing me. Can I get out of the mall through here?" he begged, pointing to the back of the arcade.

"What's a matter, dude, you lifting?"

"What are you talking about? Can I get out this way, yes or fucking no?"

"Lighten up, old fella. They going to get you for stealing?"

Quitman took a chance, "Yes, I was stealing. That's what's in this suitcase."

The teenager smiled, "To the back and to the left. It'll take you to the alley."

Quitman pushed five bucks in the kid's hand and darted away.

VanDyk crashed into the group, "You see which way he went?"

"Who?" the same kid asked.

"The guy who ran through here with the suitcase." The crowd dispersed in silence. VanDyk took off running toward the exit. His stride flowed natural and even, his breathing rhythmic.

Quitman wedged himself behind a dumpster and slumped against the brick wall. He wiped the sweat from his brow as his rapid breathing was punctuated by coughing. He hadn't counted on the unpredictable qualities of human behavior when the stakes got high enough. He never imagined Hackett with a gun, yet moments ago there he stood, steadfast and determined, in a crowd of hundreds of people, aiming a gun at the bridge of Quitman's nose, dead blind to the world around him. He hadn't counted on VanDyk either, the igneous stare that made him feel already dead, deep in the territory of that otherworld with its gleaming steel door slammed shut behind him. He had the money and the coin; how long did he have to live? Everyday life was a walk in paradise compared to this, he thought.

❦

"Hackett? Emile Hackett?" Not waiting for the uniform's reply, Fresh pushed past, ducked under the yellow barrier tape, and hurried to the fountain. "Are there any witnesses?" He glanced over either shoulder. "Officer, get the hell over here."

The uniform ran over. "Yes, sir."

"Were there any witnesses?"

"Yes, Sir."

"I want to talk to them."

"Now?"

Fresh rubbed his hand over his face, then jammed it into his pocket. "Yes, fucking now. Get a hold of mall security and have this wing sealed off. No one in, no one out. I want everyone asked what they saw and what they heard, not, repeat, not *if* they heard or saw anything. Do you understand me?"

She nodded.

Fresh looked down at the floating torn face being struck by the fountain's spray. Each drop of water diffused the blood, diluting the red to pink. "Get this fountain shut off," he hollered.

He knelt on the fountain's edge, reached in and retrieved the fragmented gun. Holding it between two gentle fingers, by the trigger guard, he couldn't tell if it had exploded in firing, or been demolished by the impact of a much larger shell's strike. He laid it back beside the body.

It was nine hours later when the last of the witnesses finally got to leave and Fresh finally got to review his notes. According to them, the man with Hackett had been either tall or short, fat or thin, white or black, blond, redhead, brunette, or bald. Many agreed on one point though: Hackett's companion appeared scared to death.

Fifteen

Quitman opened the suitcase. Even in death Hackett had the ability to surprise him. "Newspaper! Fuck you, you dead son-of-a-bitch," he rasped. He didn't care about the money, he just wanted to have it. A way to count who was winning. A way to buy back the unbuyable lives of Helen and Marty. He wished Hackett was alive so he could kill him.

σ

The parking lot was nearly empty, tinged green by halogen lights. VanDyk was out there somewhere, Quitman was sure of that. It was a lot of area to cover, ten city blocks. With a little luck, VanDyk would be wandering around some other part of it. Quitman stepped out from the enclosure, looked left then right then left again, as though he was crossing a street, more wary of things on his blind side, then strode briskly toward his car. Every twenty steps or so he spun to walk backward. Sweat crept down the sides of his shirt, though a chill walked his shoulders. His steps sounded like crushing crepe paper in the silence, his car an illusion that seemed to draw farther away the more he walked. He knew no matter what he did now, even if he gave the coin to VanDyk, he knew too much. Wish I didn't know now what I didn't know then, he thought. He was no longer a bystander, an innocent, inconvenient slug. He'd elevated himself from that lowly stature to that of a target, an error that needed correcting. He moved quickly now.

The cold steel of the driver's door handle had barely entered his grasp when he saw VanDyk, not twenty yards away, running toward him. "The fuck. Dammit," Quitman cursed and ran straight at him. The collision toppled both men to the ground. Quitman struggled to his feet.

"Give me the coin and I'll let you go," VanDyk said as he rose.

"Why should I believe that?"

They stalked each other in a wide circle.

"I got no use for you," VanDyk said, closing the gap.

"Exactly." Quitman charged, stopped cold by a brutal right fist that sank him to his knees. He staggered up and lunged at VanDyk, whose right fist landed on almost the identical spot as his previous blow. A storm of white-hot dots exploded before Quitman's eyes. He felt himself being hoisted by the lapels and spun around, stopped suddenly by crashing into the metal body of the car.

"Give me the coin."

Oddly, Quitman felt a spark of satisfaction in knowing he had read VanDyk right. Killing someone wasn't enough for him. He needed the submission of his victim first; he needed to know he had conquered, not merely won. Quitman saw the blur of VanDyk's face through his half-shut eyes, the enormous fist drawing back. This would be the last he'd remember, he knew that. With all the breath he could draw, he spat a mouthful of bloody slime at the face.

The bang! rang so loud that at first he thought it issued from inside his own head. He went limp and dropped to the asphalt. VanDyk was already lying there.

He looked up. Maria stood with her feet in a wide stance, her muscular legs flexed, gun held in both hands, arms extended, elbows locked, silhouetted by the greenish lot lights.

Coughing, spitting blood, dazed like a fighter who can't even count the fingers before his face, he rolled onto his haunches.

"What the hell are you doing here?" She lowered the gun. He tossed the car keys to her. "Unlock the trunk. We gotta get him out of here." He wrestled onto all fours. "Can you hear me, Stevie? Move, will you?" he managed to ask just before his lungs and abdomen retched and the splat of his vomit hit the ground.

Dead bodies are like bags of sand. No matter what part you lift, the weight shifts to the other end, like picking up a slinky by one end. They finally got it in the trunk, crunched down the legs, tucked in the hands. She drove. Quitman viewed the world through a fly's eyes, faceted lenses with whirling images, blurring and focusing haphazardly. His cheek felt like raw liver.

Maria was frightened until she realized that he wasn't choking, he was laughing. "You see something funny here?"

"No. I don't know, I just feel happy. My head feels the size of a hot-air balloon, my fucking face is hot enough to cook on, and I'm not really sure if I'm goddamned blind or not cause nothing's ever looked this way before. But it's naked flesh in touch with the elements. I'm alive. Ugly as fuck, but alive."

"O'Neil, do you have to swear like that?"

"Jesus. I don't believe you. You just killed a man,

point-blank, and you're worried about swearing?"

"I didn't kill a man, O'Neil. I saved one."

"A grateful one," he said. He looked in her direction, but didn't need his eyes to see, he envisioned her in the tingling in his groin.

○

They had driven up Palm to Kalmia. They took the frontage road heading south and pulled into the first small motel they came to that looked like it had working toilets. The black night surrounded them. A swarm of bugs battered themselves against the neon sign and smaller congregations attacked the light bulbs in the walkway overhangs. The small room was done in rust colors, a reddish on the carpet and drapes, a faded orange on the bedspread and chair.

"Hold still. I almost poked your eye out."

"It stings."

She mothered him with jibes. "Haven't you ever seen a John Wayne movie? Stoic bravery. Never show you're hurting? Bite down on the wooden stick, or the bullet. Seriously, try to be still."

"I didn't believe it then and I sure as hell don't believe it now. John Wayne was just an actor making believe he was hurt. There's a big difference between making believe you're hurt and this. Ow."

"I'm almost done. Try to hold still." He was lying on the bed, his head cradled in her arms. The good side of his face rested on her ample bosom. "What do we do next?"

"What the hell were you doing there, anyway?" The astringent on his wounds had an acrid odor, pleasant but firm.

"I was following you."

"Why?"

"You'd done so well at losing the police, there wasn't anyone to watch your back."

"Thanks."

"There. I'm done. You'll feel twinges of this for a month."

"Twinges I could stand."

"The headache'll go away in four, maybe five days. Try to take it easy."

He stood, then sat quickly. "I don't have four or five days."

"You need sleep now, not later."

"What did we pass on the way here?"

"Fast food, a hardware store, doughnut shop, I don't remember what else. Why?"

"Walk to the hardware, get some gloves. Was it a big one?"

"Yes."

"They'll have work shirts and jeans, get me some. And an ice chest, small one."

*

She got the night clerk to call a taxi. The cab's lights threw long beams into the mist of the near-vacant lot. "That's my car over there," she said, leaning forward over the seat and pointing, "the four-door."

"You're lucky it's still here. Shouldn't leave it in places like this."

"Oh I know. Thanks for the advice."

She agonized over the tip. There was enough about this ride to make it memorable—the hour, the location—without adding more. The driver kept his lights focused on the car until she was inside and he saw it start.

At the first deserted corner, she pulled over to the curb. Walking around to the front of the car, she bent down and flipped the gun into the sewer.

The brush of her fingers on his forehead woke him. Anxiety caromed through his mind at the sight of unfamiliar surroundings and it took a moment for his mind to jigsaw together the events that led him here. The tension in his body slackened.

"Are you alright?" she asked, continuing to stroke his head.

"Yeah, just confused for a moment." Saliva formed in his mouth, releasing the rotting smell of dried blood on his gums. "Shit, you got any mouthwash? Gum? Anything?"

"I've got some gum, I think." She hefted her purse to her knees and, sitting there pigeon-toed, she rummaged through the Kleenex and unpaid bills, the make-up kit and a hundred other mysteries. "Here it is." She dusted the silt of purse-bottom make-up from the package and extended it to him.

The pain of bringing his teeth together bolted up his cheek, through his eye, and out across his temple into his hairline. "Jesus," he said, chewing tentatively, his hand on his jaw, helping it work, "how long have I been sleeping?"

" 'Bout eight hours."

"That bastard must be starting to reek by now. We gotta get rid of him."

"Then what?" she asked, shifting her weight on the bed, leaning back on her elbows and shaking out her damp hair.

"There's still one left to get even with," Quitman began. "When I think about him I think, could he know what he's done? How could he and still have done it? I mean from the time I was sixteen, when my parents died until just a couple of years ago I had no idea what I was doing, where I was going. Nothing. Then suddenly things just fell into place. My life was marked out. The signposts were all there. My parents were still dead; that's a stupid thing to say, isn't it? Of course they were still dead, what else? What I mean is one day it just stopped being an anomaly. I stopped waking up in the morning expecting to see them or for them to be there, and I started waking up in the morning expecting to remember them. To think of them. They stopped being a part of my real life and became a part of my reality instead. Does this make any sense? I'm rambling. Anyhow." He threw an arching glance around the room, as though his eyes followed an imagined rainbow. "Anyhow. Here I am again. Same place, new players. I wake up expecting certain things that I know for a fact aren't true, certain people that, I know don't exist, I'm expecting to be there. I think of something that might have made Helen laugh and her phone number comes with it part and parcel, or I hear someone talking Spanish and I think, Marty could sell him . . . I'm going to get that son-of-a-bitch somehow."

"Then what?"

"I don't know, 'Then what,' I don't know. Look for my peace of mind again. I just hope it doesn't take another eight fucking years."

"You have some control over that."

"So you tell me . . . I don't even know what he looks like, this Lyman. I've never even seen him and he's running my life. I think about him all the time."

"I know what he looks like. I even know where he lives."

"How?"

"After you told me about him I went and looked him up. I'm a cop's daughter, remember?" She sprang forward from her reclined position to her purse; she extracted a pack of cigarettes. "He's frog-ugly, if you ask me. Looks like one. Big, broad rear end and a head that looks like it's been scrunched down, you know, and it swelled out at the sides from the pressure."

"I didn't know you smoked."

"Haven't had one in months. That's how old these are. Just sounded good."

"Let me have one." Quitman feared that first puff would make him cough. It didn't. It tasted surprisingly good. "You know where he lives, we could plant the gun there."

"No, we couldn't," she said, letting the smoke drift from her mouth uninhaled. "I threw it in the sewer this morning. Anyway it was registered to me."

"Can't they still tell something from the bullet?"

"Not likely. Not that size of slug in the head. It needs to pass through soft tissue or be lodged there. All that bone destroys it."

"Christ, you grew up gruesome."

She crushed out her cigarette. "I don't know about you, O'Neil. Your outlook is strange. It's not gruesome, it's just the facts of life."

"Whenever I think of the facts of life, I think about the birds and bees."

"There you go again."

"Yeah, there I go again." He sat on the edge of the bed, his forehead against his palm. The cigarette burned idle between his fingers. Without lifting his head or moving his eyes, he said, "I got it. I got it. The one irreversible proof."

"What?"

"Fingerprints."

Sixteen

He didn't close the door when he came back into the room. "I'll wash up, and then you follow me, okay?"

"Sure," she said, stuffing things into her purse.

She was still unfamiliar with the borrowed four-door so she found it difficult to keep up as she followed his zigzag path back to the mall. It made her appreciate how difficult it is to follow someone in a car. Even now, when the other driver knew she was there and was taking some precautions not to lose her, he had to pull over more than once when he made a light that she didn't. The parking lot teemed with people in the failing light of early evening, just before the automatic lighting kicked in. Quitman and Maria waited in their separate cars, fifty yards apart. He waited for the same parking space, the one next to the puddle of blood—although it looked more like the dried sticky mess of a melted popsicle. The interior of Quitman's car reeked of death. Quitman felt no remorse, it was more a sense of smallness, a pang of isolation at knowing what one tiny piece of metal could do. A shock at the sight of a man who a day ago was fierce and cruel and deadly, now lying still and shrunken. He must've died instantly, Quitman thought and then he wondered if instant death was anything like instant pudding, not all that instant after all.

Finally the space he waited for was available. He zoomed his car into the spot and killed the engine. He wiped down the steering wheel one last time and slid out, dragging the ice chest behind him. He looked around. No one was paying any particular attention to him as they passed by him on their way to the mall. He wiped down the keys on the tail of his new flannel shirt and popped open the trunk. The burning energy of death rushed into his nostrils. He flung the keys inside and walked away from its open yawn.

"Where to now?"

He lifted the ice chest over the seat and put it in the rear. "Someplace to watch, Stevie. A bar would be nice."

❦

Brutes grunted across two hundred diagonal inches of television screen at the far end of the room. The football was as big as a toddler hurtling through the air in a forward pass and the crowd screamed and shrieked at every play.

"You come here often?" Quitman asked Maria.

"Used to. This place is notorious for serving minors. The high school crowd loves it. My girlfriends and I practiced what to say before we came in here the first time. There we were—you have to picture this if you're going to enjoy it, so try." She touched his hand across the table, "Come on, try."

He smiled back, turned his palm up and held her hand gently in his. "Okay."

"There we were, eight of us, crammed in my tiny bedroom at home, when I lived with my parents, practicing how to be natural. You know, how to sound like we'd said it a million times before. 'I'll have a beer.' I mean most of us lowered our voices trying to sound more mature, or something. Then one of the other girls would say, 'What kind?' and we'd answer 'Bud, please, a Bud's fine.' As if they wouldn't know when eight seventeen-year-old girls came in and all said exactly the same thing, one after another. We were just too young to realize that they'd've served us no matter what we said. Girls our age were an attraction."

"No kidding."

"Oh, don't make fun of me. Don't you think that story's cute?"

"I do," he said, kneading her fingers. "What would you like now? Would a Bud be fine?"

"A Scotch would be better."

"I'll be right back."

Quitman squeezed himself into a space at the bar. He heard the crowd shriek and turned to watch. In the slow-motion replay, two bodies collided, their twisted wreckage crumpling to the ground in a heap. "Two Scotch and soda, when you got a second," he called out in the ensuing hush of afterplay. Now if the spectators all lit a cigarette at once it would be just like sex, he thought.

*

Maria sipped at her third drink. Moments ago, the game had ended and the crowd poured out of the bar. All that remained were a few regulars roosting on their regular stools at the final curve of the bar. One bartender, the older of the two, stood chatting with them, while the other one restocked the beer cases and back bar. The two waitresses wiped tables and stacked extra chairs. The stale smell of years of spilled beer hung in the air. Other than that the room was deserted except for Quitman and Maria.

"Did you love her, O'Neil?"

"I don't know. I was feeling something. My brand of love, I suppose."

"You start every answer with 'I don't know,' did you know that?"

"Maybe," he caught himself before he said it again, "I'm not sure, you could be right."

"I am right. Take my word for it."

"What's the difference?"

"I was just wondering if you loved her."

"I told you, I don't know. Besides, whatever I felt before she was killed is too muddled now by what I feel since she's been killed. I don't know who I'm sorrier for, her or me. Could have been love, or something more like selfishness. Maybe my kind of love is nothing more than selfishness. I need time to sort it out."

"Isn't love selfishness?"

"Save it for college, Stevie. The fuck would I know?"

"Do you think I'm attractive, O'Neil? I mean, in my own sort of way?"

He eyed her bold face. The strong jaw, the abundant hair, helter-skelter about her face. "Yes," he said, though he didn't really mean it, so he added, "striking is a better word."

"Thanks." She tasted her drink again. "Can I ask you something?"

"Sure."

"Why haven't you tried to make love to me, I mean recently?"

"Would it really be a matter of trying?"

"You know what I mean."

"Not a hundred percent."

"Half the time when I talk to you I'd just as soon strangle you, you know that?"

"Likewise, I'm sure."

"You're infuriating."

"Thanks." He grinned.

"Every other man I've spent any time with wants to get me in bed. You don't seem to want anything."

"We've been in bed together."

"I know. That makes it even harder to understand."

"It's easier to make love to strangers," he shrugged.

"What does that mean?"

"At least with a stranger, there's a possibility. How can you have love at first sight with someone you already know?"

"Thanks a lot," she huffed.

"That's not what I mean. I don't know what I mean. I mean I'm looking for love that's a miracle."

"God, you're a romantic but you're practical, too. A little too practical about it. Otherwise you'd understand that every sight is first sight."

"And?"

"What isn't attractive about me?"

"Do we really have to do this?"

"Humor me."

"I didn't say you weren't attractive."

"Then what's not to love? Come on, I feel like being personal. I need someone to talk to and," her tongue dripped a little sarcasm, "God help me, you're all that's available right now."

"Hey, if I think about it, it's probably me that I don't think I could love right now, alright?"

"I feel like a melon rind on someone's discarded plate." She frowned.

"It's probably VanDyk."

"You think so?" She slumped back in her chair. They sat silent for a moment. She concentrated on her glass as she rotated it in her strong fingers. "You know what I really feel like? I feel like the first time I got fucked."

Quitman snickered, "The first time you what?"

"Got fucked."

"I didn't think you knew those kind of words."

"Oh, everybody knows 'those kind of words,' Quitman. Anyway that's what it was. Fucked. God knows how bad I wanted it. I loved him and he loved me, I think. I think he even thought that he loved me. I think that once we decided to do it I was just one big receptacle to him and the sooner he got it in and over with the better. It was over before I knew it started as far as I was concerned. Neither of us could look the other in the face. I wanted to talk about it, but I didn't know what to say. It was just in the energy of the room or something that we should both be quiet.

"You know what he told me? A few days later, you know what he said? He told me he was studying the Australopitho-something-or-other, in Anthro, some kind of early human from Africa, he told me that the professor had said that upright walking contributed to development of early society not so much by freeing the hands for work but by rearranging the skeletal structure in such a way that early humans could copulate face-to-face and that created a sense of responsibility unknown prior to that and allowed for sexual involvement to become a form of play. So, I thought, this is how he says, 'I love you.'

"I quit school and came home. Sounds crazy, I know—" With the room nearly empty each sound was magnified. She spoke intentionally lower so that it wouldn't echo in the vast room. "Did you ever go to college, O'Neil?"

"Yes. It's the one asset my parents didn't liquefy, so to speak. My father believed in education. There was an endowment."

She shifted in her seat, ill at ease with the question she

asked next, "Why are you a car salesman? Forgive me but, I don't know how else to ask."

"You think there's something wrong with it?"

"Not really, it just doesn't seem to fit."

"Well, we've got some time to kill, what the hell, huh?" he began. He finished his drink and waved at the bartender for a refill, looked at her glass and gestured for two instead of one. "I really like school so don't get me wrong on that. It's one of the best times of my life, just like everybody always tells their kids. When I graduated, no matter how many papers I looked through there were no ads for Liberal Artists in the classifieds. Far as I could tell I'd done everything right. I got an education, even got that little ribbon, the 'with distinction' one, on the corner of my degree. I had volunteer experience, club experience, student government, just about everything but it wasn't getting me a job. I was down at the library one day making a list of more places to send my resume so I could, hopefully, one day, quit my minimum-wage campus job, when this guy comes in and sits at the same table with me. He's got nothing in front of him. He didn't bring anything with him to the table to look at. He just sat there and stared, for a long time, at the book stack across from us, it was in reference, it was the phone books. You know, from all over the country. He sat there about ten minutes then he got up and grabbed the directory for Hawaii. I couldn't help it, I had to ask him what he was doing."

The waitress brought the drinks. Quitman and Maria clicked the glasses before sipping. "Well, to shorten this up a little. . . . "

"I'm not bored," she said, smiling.

"Whatever. When I told him what I was doing he pulled out his wallet and slid this single piece of paper toward me. I opened it and it was a W-2 form. He'd made a hundred thousand the year before. He pointed to the top and said, that shows I worked for a car dealer and this code number next to it shows I was a salesman. Now I'm going to Hawaii and I'll have a job within one hour of those fat jet tires hitting the tarmac. The rest . . . "

She stopped him mid-sentence. "O'Neil, look," she urged, casting her round eyes toward the television. Their abandoned Buick had made the eleven o'clock news.

☙

The atrium of Lyman's office building hosted a cluster of small restaurants. Quitman ordered a pizza to go and took the elevator to the seventh floor.

Henry Lyman's secretary was adamant, but so was he. "What do you mean you didn't order it? Look, I'm just trying to make a buck, you got something against people trying to make a living? They told me seven twelve downstairs. You want to call them? Maybe your boss ordered and didn't tell you. You know everything? Call him out here, ask him. Is that a problem? Is he a king or what, can't answer a simple question for a guy who's just trying to make a living? I got rights, too, you know. . . . "

"What's the trouble here?"

Quitman spun toward the voice. Lyman filled the doorway. Hips as broad as his shoulders. Icy eyes peered through slits in the very white skin of his face, a man who can wish someone dead and have his wishes come true. Clear-skinned and blameless as a child.

"Is there a problem, young man?"

Frozen, transfixed, Quitman struggled to free himself. "Ah, um," he shook his head, haltingly. "Is this your pie? Didn't you order a pizza?" he asked, gesturing wildly with his free hand. "When you order, you ought to let your girl here know, know what I mean?"

"Young man, I did not order a pie, as you put it, today. Nor would I order one any day, for that matter. We have work to do here, if it doesn't inconvenience you." Lyman swung his hand to indicate the exit.

"You mean this isn't yours? Shit. Fuck, man. Shit-fuck, what am I going to do with it? It's cold now. That asshole downstairs'll take it out of my pay. What then? Fuck."

Lyman strode across the room and flung the outer door open. "Get out of this office immediately."

Quitman felt the draft of the slamming door on the nape of his neck. At the elevator, he opened the box and removed a slice; the cheese was rich with the aroma of olives. He stuffed a big bite into his mouth as the elevator door opened. He wedged himself in.

"Can you imagine that?" he said to no one in particular. "The prick doesn't even like pizza."

❧

"You want some pizza?" he asked her, as he slid into the car and laid the box between them. She tore off a slice, holding one hand cupped under the tip to catch any drips or spills.

"What's Lyman's house like?" he asked her.

"Exurban." She brushed a dot of tomato sauce from the corner of her mouth. "Maybe I should say mountainous, even farther out and up. It's about twenty miles from here. Want to go?"

"You bet. Tell me more."

"It's stone front, kind of far back from the road, up one of the canyons."

"Anything going on? You know, activity. He married, do you think?"

"You've seen him. Hard to imagine, isn't it?"

"Can't tell about tastes."

"There's no evidence of children. God. Could you picture that? What kids of his would look like?"

"No. But what about a wife?"

"Well, it was late afternoon, about five, and there was still mail in the mailbox, so even if he is married, she could work, too. Or at least be out a lot, you know, spending money. Even if he is married she's not home, I'll bet on that."

"Anything else?"

"Are you done with this pizza? If you are, I'll put it in the back, otherwise I'll just keep eating it. It goes right to my hips. God, I shouldn't eat this kind of stuff at all. There's planters lining the front. You know, those brick things that everyone's so crazy about now? Filled with pansies. Lots of color. It's beautiful, really."

"Pansies, huh? Keep a look out for a nursery."

The big four-door lumbered along the monotonous highway. "Driving this thing is like driving a living room or one of my father's cruisers. I have to keep telling myself that I'm the driver so that I don't forget and go to sleep or something," she said.

"You know, before this, I never had any contact with the police, outside of traffic. It must be really different to grow up within that kind of structure, that kind of family."

"To a child it's just like any other kind of family, really. . . . Oh look, there's a nursery down over there," she said, gliding the steamship of a car across the lanes and onto the exit ramp.

❡

"We might have some in the back," the nurseryman apologized, "but if we do they've all but gone to seed. I

168

don't really recommend planting this late in the season. It'll be a miracle if they come through the winter."

"I'll take the chance. Check and see, will you?"

The nurseryman came back lugging two flats. "See? I'd be embarrassed to sell these."

"I don't mind. I'll take them."

Exasperated, the clerk said, "If you must, just take them. I couldn't accept money."

"You could sell me a shovel, couldn't you?" Quitman said. "Stevie, pay the man."

Seventeen

Stevenson walked around his desk, distancing himself from Fresh. "I don't know what's going on here and I don't like the feeling. One man blows the life out of himself with a filthy gun, and another has his face literally shot away, his hands hacked off his body, and he's stuffed in the trunk of a car. Both these killings take place within four hundred yards of each other and within hours of each other and we've got nothing?"

"You said it yourself, we've got nothing," Fresh smirked enigmatically.

"Nothing to identify the man in the trunk?"

"No face, no hands; we don't have a corpse. All we have is a body." Fresh shifted in his chair, balancing the stack of files in his lap.

"The man in the fountain was Emile Hackett. He's associated with O'Neil, isn't he? I need something beside excuses. I put this ball in your court. Can't we point to O'Neil on this?"

"You mean frame him?"

"No," Stevenson said cautiously, "but he's in this, isn't he?"

"If you don't mean implicate him, then I don't know what the hell you do mean," Fresh snapped. "I never thought you were like this."

"What the hell do you mean by that?" Stevenson demanded, his face flushing.

"I couldn't believe it, just a week ago, when the media and the mayor were fighting for space on your back, you turned around and dumped this on me, put it 'in my court,' isn't that the way you just phrased it? You handed this pile of files to me and walked away with both hands over your ass." Fresh jumped up, scattering the files across the office floor.

"What are you going to do in your next career? Pick up those goddamn files!"

"Listen. I don't know who the body in the trunk belongs to, I don't know why Hackett died, I don't know who brutalized Helen Costello and, for fucking what it's worth, I don't even have any idea who killed Jorgé Martinez. But if you want an implication I've got one you're going to love." Fresh drew a deep breath and fired, "That faceless, handless corpse, that was beginning to rot when we found it, was doing it in a car registered to a friend of O'Neil's . . . one Maria Stevenson. I think if you dig through those files on your floor there, you'll probably recognize the address. I know the name's familiar."

"What?" Stevenson shouted, a tic taking control of the corner of his right eye.

"It's in your daughter's name. Paperwork, everything. Paid cash. It was in the glove compartment. Want to talk 'next careers'? I'll leave this up to you."

"Why wasn't I told of this? Where do you get off trying to protect me?"

Fresh felt that somehow he'd landed in a dream. That the man he was in the room with, Homicide Chief Stevenson, bore no relation to the man he had come to the force with many years ago. He rubbed his hands over his face in wistful despair. "Are you from another planet, for chrissake? I came to this department about the same time as a guy who looks exactly like you, even had the same name, but that's where it ends. Why the hell would anybody want to protect you? I was trying to protect her. And from what? From the law? The consequences? Fuck no. I was protecting her from *you*. I was protecting her from anymore of what you call love. That cold, dispassionate way you treat her. You haven't forgiven her for the last 'mistake' she made and that was more than a decade ago. And what the hell was her crime then, can you tell me that? Being born female, was that it? You know how many times she asked me how to get you to love her again? No, Sir, Chief of Detectives Stevenson, I sure as hell wasn't trying to protect your cold, worthless ass. You can put money on that."

Stevenson slumped into his chair. The room swirled around him. All the solidity of his existence vaporized. He shuddered. "Who else knows?" he mumbled.

"No one." Fresh, satisfied though sorrowful, bent and began to scoop the files from the floor.

"Leave those. Leave me alone for awhile."

When Fresh shut the door behind him Stevenson slowly turned his chair to face the documents and photos, a history of a failed and forgotten civilization.

He put his hands to his face. He felt the sweat on his brow, his tongue rasped against the ash-dry roof of his mouth. He pushed himself up, propped by a hand on his desk, his knees uncertain. He drew methodical breaths. He gathered the files, stacking them neatly, distant from the task but capable.

*

"Tell him it's O'Neil, Quitman O'Neil. Spell it anyway you like, he'll recognize the name. Tell him to meet me at Mickey's. It's a sports bar over on Seventh. About nine o'clock. Tell him maybe I can give him a hand."

As soon as he replaced the receiver in the cradle the phone rang. "Let me answer that," Maria called.

He backed up, making room for her to wedge between him and the counter. He felt the brush of her hips against his groin, inhaled the musk of her wet hair.

She propped the receiver against her shoulder. "Hello." She continued to towel out her hair. "Oh hi, Daddy, how are you?" She beetled her eyebrows, listening. "No. I'm fine, really. Is something wrong?" She laid the towel on the counter, switched the phone to her other ear, "It's nice to hear your voice, too; I talked to Mom last night, did she tell you?"

Quitman walked to the window at the far end of the living room as Maria spoke into the phone. The gray sky hung low. The air grew a chill and stirred dust in erratic eddies. Cars glided by silently in the street below. The suction of a passing truck gave flight to a sheet of newspaper that somersaulted effortlessly before gluing itself to the grill of the next car to pass. Melancholy swept over him, a sudden stab that bypassed his brain and shot right into his central nervous system. He kept looking out the window, no longer seeing anything in particular. Only her voice unlocked his reverie.

"That was weird," she said, coming up behind him, wrapping her hair in the towel turban-style.

"Weird how?"

"He sounded so, I don't know, lost I suppose. It's not like him to call. He usually has my mother do it if he wants me to come over or something." She sat across from Quitman and undid the turban and toweled the ends of her hair between her hands like someone making ropes out of clay.

"He started talking about when I was younger," she began. "I don't think I ever told you about this but when

173

I was a kid I trained in gymnastics. Not just did gymnastics but trained. Like six or seven hours a day." Her eyes widened for emphasis. "That's seven days a week. He talked about just before the accident, about our plans, about the events we'd already won. . . . We were a team, you know that? I'd forgotten that; but we were a team, my dad and me."

She stopped drying her hair and looked off into the middle distance with a glimmer of wonder in her eyes. "He talked about Europe. Now that's been a forbidden subject forever." The glimmer turned to a tear. "He said he missed me. He hasn't said anything like that to me since I don't remember when. . . . You know what else he said?"

"No," Quitman answered.

"He said he felt like he hadn't been paying enough attention to me and did I think he was neglecting me." She returbaned her hair and pulled her legs up under her and sat idol-like and erect. "He hasn't paid any real attention to me, except to be sure I wasn't sullying the family somehow, in a dozen years. Can you imagine that, a dozen?"

"What do you suppose caused that?" Quitman asked.

"I don't know," she said, wiping away the tears of her confusion. "Anyway, he said he was talking to some of the guys around the station about travel. He said he realized that travelling could be important to my education. He said he realized suddenly that I should have gone to Europe years ago. Even if not with the gymnastics thing then just for the sake of going for goings sake. I deserved it then and I still deserved it now, he said. Can you believe it?" She put her fingers to her cheeks and breathed deeply, composing herself. "He asked if I still would be interested, if I still wanted to go to Europe. Can you imagine that?" She kept saying "Can you imagine that?"

because she was having difficulty imagining it herself. "He had an absolute fit when I went away to Marquette for my freshman year, and now he wants me to go to Europe?"

"Maybe he sees you're grown up."

"Oh come on."

"Maybe. You never know, he might. Lots of things that take years to happen only take a second to realize."

"You know one of the things I like about you, O'Neil? You don't judge. I think inside yourself you sympathize or empathize but you don't get that horrible puppy-dog look of pity in your eyes when I tell you something. You just sit there, and you honestly seem to be listening."

And so that's what Quitman did then, just listened.

They sat quiet for several moments before she said, "He asked about you."

"What did you tell him?"

"That I hadn't seen you."

"Maybe he knows something."

"Like what?" she asked.

"Like that you shot VanDyk."

"Nonsense. How could he know that?"

"I don't know."

"Me neither. Besides, he just asked about you in passing. His mind was somewhere else, don't ask me where. You ever been to Europe, O'Neil?"

"Nope. I've never even been to Florida, for chrissake, or Maine. Why would I go to Europe? America first, you know?"

"I don't know, I just asked."

He mixed two drinks, strong on Scotch. "So you'd go?" Quitman asked.

Maria shrugged, still numbed with delight by her father's offers; the trip and the reconciliation. "Yes, why not? Yes, of course. Europe, God, can you imagine that?" she said, grinning with joy.

"It'd be good, you need to distance yourself from this, from here, for awhile." He saw something come over her, a calm wave of contained happiness. It wormed his own sense of melancholy deeper into his heart. "Your father sounds like an alright type."

She fidgeted with some papers on the counter. Her growing excitement glowed on her cheeks. "He's had his times in the past and maybe those days are coming back. I hope so. I wish he were here so I could hug him. God, Europe!" she exclaimed, leaping over to Quitman's chair and hugging him in proxy.

He was the one to end the embrace. He stood with his hand on the doorknob. "I have to go."

"Wait," she said, "I have something for you." She got her purse and rummaged through it, finally coming up with an over-under Derringer. "Take this. Please?"

"So you do have a trinket-type after all."

"Huh?"

"Nothing really. I don't have much use for guns."

"It would make me feel better. Take it," she said, extending it to him on her open palm.

He slid it into his pants pocket. It added very little weight to the keys already in there. "Thanks."

After a pause he continued, "I have to meet Fresh. I really don't know what to say without its being maudlin. I owe you a lot. Maybe it's just the moment. Maybe I'm feeling overdramatic or something, I don't know. Maybe because there's a better than good chance we'll never . . . I just don't know what to say."

She tiptoed and kissed his cheek. He saw the glassy sheen of her eyes. She said. "Good-bye and good luck."

"You have a way with words," he said, closing the door behind him.

The whirr turned to a hiss as Stevenson fed the sheets, one at a time, into the shredder's mouth. He worked in the back of the copy room, in the dark. There were three thick files on the table beside him. The Martinez file, the Costello file, and one they called the M/C/O link file; M for Martinez, C for Costello, O for O'Neil. Sheet-by-sheet he fed the entire M/C/O link file into the blades. He had to; before the S for Stevenson was added. After all, if O'Neil wasn't purged from the equation could Maria fail to appear in the result? How had she become involved in this? Why hadn't she come to him, her father, for help? Though Fresh hadn't said as much, she must have asked him. Fresh wouldn't have done it otherwise. If he'd have been asked, if she'd have come and said, "Daddy, please . . ." what exactly would he have done? How would he have responded to her? Would he have disappointed her as badly as he disappointed himself? What would free him from the shame of his failures, he wondered. Why was a corpse found, reeking, in the trunk of her car? How did she come to own a Buick? The more his curiosity piqued, the more his love for her curtailed his eyes. No one would question what he was doing there in the dark. He could be in there in the dark or with the lights blazing, he just felt more comfortable in the gloom. Just barely seeing his hands lifting the sheets. He thought they could have been anybody's hands, couldn't they?

Eighteen

Henry Lyman entered his house through the garage. He pushed a button to cause the garage door to rumble shut and another to flicker on the fluorescent in the kitchen. He placed his briefcase on the floor by the doorway and took the two steps down to the sunken tile floor.

He popped open the liquor cabinet. The magnetic door released with a faint click. He splashed brandy into a snifter glass, drew a cigar from the humidor, and sniffed the length of it, trimmed the tip and lit it slowly, puffing small clouds of smoke from the side of his mouth. He held a puff in his mouth, took a swill of brandy and swallowed, blowing the smoke out his nose, enjoying the flooding scent in his sinuses.

He switched on no more lights, finding his way through the house by habit. Across the deep carpet, around the Duncan Phyfe in the dining room, jogging slightly to miss the corner of the low-hanging chandelier. He placed his drink on the side table in the front hall. When he pulled open the front door to retrieve his mail, something thumped him lightly on the chest. "What the . . . " Shaken, he grabbed the handle of the shovel and lifted it to the moonlight. "Damn that Chang!" he grumbled, and he continued to curse his gardener as he carried what he thought was a forgotten shovel to the garage.

❦

Quitman eeled through the packed room at Mickey's and up to the bar just in time to get the stool of someone who was being eighty-sixed for spilling his fourth drink in a row. The walls were plastered with bright fluorescent signs that read, BUCK-A-BUD NITE. Two bartenders and three waitresses darted around, falling further behind demand with every step. The jukebox blared, barely topping the din of the chatter. Quitman took his first sip just as he spied Fresh working his way through.

"What the hell happened to you?" Fresh asked, staring at the bruised flesh surrounding Quitman's eyes.

"I walked into a door."

"I'll bet." Fresh shook his head. "We're supposed to carry on a conversation in here?" He pointed to his ears.

"You get used to it. Want a beer?"

"Sure."

Quitman failed to get the attention of either bartender. "They'll be here in a minute."

"What's this about?"

"I've got your last link."

"Who?"

"Henry Lyman. If I were you, I'd dig in his flowers. May turn something up. . . . If you're nice maybe he'll let you use his new shovel."

"You and your riddles . . . but why? Why would he be involved in any of this?"

"Ask him," Quitman shrugged.

"I'm asking you. And another thing, how would he have a car registered to Maria Stevenson?"

"You buy a car for cash, nobody cares. He could have registered it to Axl Rose. Is it im-fucking-possible for you to see your way out of this thing? You got a problem with wrapping this up?"

"I don't have a problem with wrapping this up, but I do have two other problems. One's that I'm not a witch doctor, I'm a cop. My solutions can't come out of some boiling cauldron. The other's figuring out what in the hell started this in the first place."

"Maybe you're not a witch doctor, but you have to start somewhere, you need a premise. You know as well as I do that if you work with a S.I.S.O. system you get what you deserve: If it's shit-in it's shit-out, and that's what you've got right now: shit. This prick Lyman should pay for what he's done."

"I don't think he did anything."

"He caused all of it to happen. Let me grant you that maybe he didn't physically do any of it. Maybe, according to the law, he should go scot-fucking-free. VanDyk worked for him. Are you listening? I can put VanDyk in the car with Marty. With a little creative thinking, you can put him in the bedroom with Helen. What more do you want? Do you want to keep screwing around with this till it gets so complex and embroiled that all that happens in the end is that everyone apologizes like a pack of politicians, and just walks away smiling? Do you want to let this keep going till you never get it straight?"

"I want to know why."

"Do I have to do everything for you?"

"Like what?"

"What can I get you guys?" the bartender shouted.

"Put a tape recorder on me."

"Wire you?"

"My friend here needs a Bud, I'm fine," Quitman shouted back at the bartender. "Wire me, if that's what you call it, and I'll show you the fucking 'why.' "

"I'd never get that approved. I can't just put your life in danger."

"I don't know where you get off sometimes. You don't tell me what to do with my life. You don't 'put' or 'not put' me anywhere. You've been chasing your own tail too long. This case isn't a recipe and your job isn't a cookbook. Life is a lot more than just a series of procedures outlined by a pack of insurance men. There are risks and I'm willing to take my share. I'm going up there, to Lyman's. Want in?"

*

The night was thin wisps of mist with a slight drizzle in it. Strange weather for this time of year. It clung to the windshield, magnifying the oncoming headlights. Quitman glanced into the mirror at Fresh's lights rounding the curve a full turn-and-a-half behind him.

Lyman's house was off Skyline, at the top of Apache Canyon, on Xerxes. The houses weren't numbered. His was the last house on the north side. Quitman pulled over a hundred yards further down and tucked the car off the road. As he walked back toward the house he turned his collar to the cold. He saw Fresh pass by the junction and continue on Skyline up around the crest, out of sight.

He touched the hood of Lyman's car. Still warm. He walked up the low side of the driveway, not visible from the front windows. He rounded the side of the house, his steps cushioned in deep beds of pine needles. The drizzle erupted into rain. Large drops freed the stale dust from the dry surroundings and a gritty sweetness settled on his tongue. A pang of loneliness plucked him at the sight of the rain splashing into the vacant swimming pool. Up on the rear deck he tried the first set of French doors, then the second. The third was unlocked. He nervously checked the connection of the wire inside his shirt. He felt one pocket for the coin, and tapped the other pocket lightly for the derringer. He didn't know why he'd brought the gun along but he'd been carrying it since Maria had given it to him. It was like a charm, so he'd tapped it for luck.

Across the darkened sunken room and down the hall he saw a stripe of light outlining an almost-closed door. His shoes sank into the carpet's heavy nap as he cautiously approached it. Through the half open door he saw Lyman sitting in a wingback chair, reading a book. He pushed through the door as he spoke. "You order a pizza?"

Lyman spun in his chair. "What is this?" he demanded. "Who are you?" His eyes darted around the room as though it was unfamiliar to him, as though, in this panic of fright, something new would appear to save him.

"Seen VanDyk lately?"

Lyman glared at him through hooded eyes. Sweat peeked between the creases of his brow. His grip tightened on his book, whitening his fingernails. He shifted his bulk toward the edge of the chair. "I keep very little money in the house. I have some, you're welcome to it. Just take it and go."

"Cut the shit."

Lyman saw beyond the battered flesh and recognized the face. "It's you, the pizza man. What have I done to merit you? What is it you want? Are you insane, coming here over the price of a pizza?"

"Seen VanDyk?"

"No," Lyman said, even more confused by Quitman's presence and his knowledge of VanDyk. "This isn't where you're likely to find Mr. VanDyk. Have you tried his house?"

"He's not there. You can trust me on that."

Lyman fidgeted. He released the book, sliding it down between the cushion and the arm of his chair. His eyes blinked sporadically as he spoke. "I haven't been completely honest with you. I do have a safe. There's several thousand dollars in it." He hoisted himself, grunting, from his chair and turned toward the wall. "I'll get it for you."

"The money and the gun? Will you get them both? Doesn't everybody keep both in their safe?" Quitman said, sarcastically. "Just stay where the fuck you are. I don't want your money, at least not a lousy several thousand. Not when I've got this." Quitman flipped the 64 D onto a circular table alongside the chair. "My name's O'Neil. I'm the one you've been looking for from the beginning. I'm the one you were looking for when VanDyk killed Marty, the car salesman. You were looking for me when he killed Helen Costello. Now you've found me. Now what?"

Lyman barely heard Quitman's words. His eyes burned dryly, concentrating on the coin face. Even at arm's length he could read the date. His eyes widened. The sight of the coin mesmerized him—the reality of seeing up close what so few had ever seen. "May I sit down?" Lyman asked.

Quitman thought a moment. "Yes." Lyman headed swiftly for the chair nearest the table where the coin lay, but Quitman stopped him. "Not there. Not your favorite chair. Sit over here." He pointed to a place on the far side of the room.

Lyman's protruding eyes flashed disappointment as he seated himself. He stared longingly across the room at the 64 D, glimmering under the soft lamplight. "Surely you'll let me inspect the coin?" He couldn't imagine anyone cruel enough not to.

"Later."

The round man huffed. "Won't you join me, Mr. O'Neil?" he said, indicating the chair across from himself with deliberation. "Nothing worthwhile's ever been accomplished standing toe-to-toe." When Quitman took his seat, Lyman continued. "I like you, Mr. O'Neil. You're tenacious, I admire that in a man. I'm glad you came to me with whatever proposition you have. How can we do business?"

Quitman answered: "How can I trust you? You sent Hackett to meet with me with a gun and a suitcase full of newspapers."

When Quitman saw a wave of surprise sweep over Lyman's face, he broke out laughing. "I don't believe it, but the look on your face tells me it must be true." He leaned closer to Lyman. He saw the slick sweat on the fat man's creased and freckled eyelids, and his bulbous cheeks. "You gave Hackett the money, the two million. Double-crossing everyone was his own innovation. So now you're out two million and the only man who knows where that is is dead."

"I think you know where that is, Mr. O'Neil."

"Your guess is as good as mine."

"Why don't you just keep the money and leave me with the coin? Then we'd both be well rewarded for our efforts."

Quitman turned his palms up and quizzed, "What's wrong with you? I don't have the money. Why do you think I'm here? If I had the money, then I would have both the money and the coin. I could go anywhere in the world. Why would I be here, with you?"

Lyman's face soured. His heavy jowls sagged down,

dragging the corners of his mouth into a scowl. His eyes hardened, creasing the corpulent skin into furrows. "For even more money," he growled, "or for revenge."

Quitman felt the hot spittle of Lyman's vehemence splatter against his face. "Don't be foolish. I have nothing against you, all I want is VanDyk. He killed the woman I love. That's more important to me than any of this." Quitman leaned back in his chair. He watched the red burst of anger drain from Lyman's cheeks. "VanDyk's a liability to you now, he's killed two people, both of them can be traced directly to you."

"Even if you're right, so what?"

"He did it for you, didn't he? Killed them, I mean?" Quitman waited in the charged silence, not expecting an answer but acting as though he did. "How long before he sees the value of what he's done? How long before he becomes a lifelong liability?" He paused again but Lyman remained silent. "I can erase that liability." He rose and leaned close to Lyman's broad, sweaty jowls again. He leaned so close he felt the hot smell of excitement strike his face, rising off the obese mass of flesh. He clenched his teeth and hissed, "I'd relish it."

Lyman's cheeks quivered. "I don't understand what it is that you want from me."

Quitman stood to his full height and paced over to the table where the coin lay. "Do you want the coin?"

Lyman sat up and took notice, "Of course I do. You know I do or you wouldn't be here."

"Give me VanDyk and you get the coin."

"But I don't know where he is!" Lyman swore, "I really don't."

"But he does work for you, doesn't he?"

"He's not a regular employee, Mr. O'Neil."

"But he worked for you to locate this coin?" Quitman said, pointing to it.

"Yes, but that doesn't—"

"Did he work for you to help you locate this coin?"

"Yes, but you must understand, as an independent he was capable of independent action."

"To put it mildly . . . don't stop there, go on."

"I don't know what else to tell you, I don't know where he is. I haven't heard from him in several days."

"You really don't want this very badly, do you?" Quitman asked and he watched Lyman's greedy eyes as he slipped the coin back into his pants pocket. "Start telling me something beside 'I don't know' and 'it's not my fault' or I'm leaving. You understand? How did you find out about the coin?"

"From Hackett."

"When did VanDyk become involved?"

"From the start." Lyman pushed himself up from the chair. "Mr. O'Neil, I must have that coin. Let me hold it."

"No, talk first."

"At least put it back on the table where I can see it." When Quitman put the coin back on the table Lyman continued. "He was involved from the first, from the time of Hackett's first call to me about the coin."

"Did you send him after Marty, the car salesman?"

"No. He was following a lead he'd developed. Don't you see? Even if I'd wanted to direct his every activity it would be impossible to do so."

"But he did kill him?" Quitman said, and then quickly rephrased for the benefit of the tape. "VanDyk did kill Marty?"

"It was an accident, but yes."

"And Helen? Did VanDyk kill Helen, too?"

"Yes."

"And finally, when you knew I was meeting Hackett

you sent him to kill me, or was it just to kill the survivor of that meeting, nothing personal?"

Lyman was near pleading when he said, "I never sent him to kill anyone."

"But people still died with amazing regularity. Did you ever think about firing him and getting someone less violent? Never mind. Don't answer that, just tell me where he is."

Lyman's stance stiffened and his meaty hands formed into fists. "I don't know where he is!" he shouted. He unclenched his fists and wiped his sweaty face. "I'll buy the coin from you. We're reasonable men, we can reach an agreement."

"I want VanDyk."

"Why ask for the one thing that I don't have? Take money. You can use the money to find him."

"I want you to tell me where he is."

"Don't make this imposs—"

"Why would it be that you don't know where Van-Dyk is or how to get a hold of him?" Quitman interrupted. "I think I know the answer to that. I think I know why you're not concerned with the liability that VanDyk could become to you." He stepped irritably close to Lyman. "He's dead, isn't he? VanDyk is dead just like all the others. And you know what else? You killed him, didn't you?"

"That's absurd!"

"You killed him and you didn't have any help this time, you did it yourself."

Suddenly Lyman's large hands grasped Quitman's throat. Quitman was amazed by how quickly his opponent moved. "I want that coin," he hissed.

Quitman staggered backward under the thrust of Lyman's charge. He brought both fists straight up, breaking Lyman's hold. They slammed against the table with the coin. Quitman's knees buckled. The two men toppled to the floor demolishing a side table, scattering the shards of its glass top everywhere, and sending the coin rolling to the center of the room. "Fresh," Quitman yelled, "can you hear me? For chrissake get up here." He struggled to get his hand in his pocket for the derringer while Lyman, on top of him, kept reaching for his throat. Quitman managed to grab the compact gun but in his haste his thumb released the safety and the gun went off. The bullet burned its way along the fleshy part of his own thigh. His body jolted, throwing the fat man off of him.

"The fuck are you waiting for, Fresh?" he mumbled, while Lyman was still struggling like an inverted turtle to roll off his back, still obsessed with the coin that lay just beyond his grasping fingers.

Quitman sat holding the gun on Lyman and watching the fat man struggle, flailing his arms and legs, and, finally flipping himself face down. He tore his pants leg open at the oblong bullet hole and inspected the stinging wound. Along its three-inch length the edge was creased like dry lips and the center was beginning to form a translucent milky bubble.

He rose painfully to his own feet, "Get up, you fat prick," he demanded. He slipped the coin into his pocket.

"Outside. We're going outside, in front." He prodded the rubbery flesh with the gun barrel.

The rain had thinned back to a mist. Cushions of fog lay in the low spots, clinging to the trees halfway up their trunks. Quitman pushed Lyman out the door and limped after him. He used the pistol to point at the pansies. "Dig."

"Dig? I can't. You saw me inside. It's too hard for me

to get up and down," Lyman whined.

Quitman reached inside his shirt and unplugged the wire. When he dug his fingers into Lyman's disheveled silver hair he felt the roots, soaked in cold sweat. He jerked the head to one side and lined the gun up along the side of Lyman's fleshy cheek and fired. The bullet sped safely away but the sliding chamber shot a spike of flame up the side of Lyman's face, blackening the skin and setting his hairline briefly aflame. "Dig," Quitman yelled, pulling his head forward by the hair. "Hear me?" he demanded, poking the gun into Lyman's bulk; but the fat man still fought to stay on his feet. Quitman drew the pistol above his head and brought the butt down sharply on Lyman's back, between his shoulders, crumpling him. Steel is steel.

"Now dig down there in the dirt with your hands," Quitman reiterated, pointing to where he had replanted the pansies.

Lyman moaned, kneeling there. He rubbed at his shoulders and touched cautiously at his brow, around the singed hair.

Quitman grabbed another fistful of Lyman's hair and pulled. The blunt scent of burnt hair filled the air. "Now, do it now," he demanded. Lyman blubbered something Quitman couldn't make out as the man knelt there pawing at the muddy ground.

Quitman walked to the top of the driveway and flung the derringer across the road into the woods. He waited there as Fresh's tires made a distant pissing sound on the rain-soaked road as his car rolled around the corner from Skyline, drew up in front of Lyman's unnumbered house, and came to a stop. His synthetic soles were almost noiseless on the gravel border of the walk.

"Did you hear?"

"I heard. It's thin, though. He's only an accessory.

No living witnesses. We'll lose him. You know what the courts are like. They're not going to take the time on this. And that sound on the tape, the bang, was that a gun? Did you bring a gun up here?"

Quitman listened with a detachment bordering on disdain. "You call in for help?"

"You hear me? There isn't enough. I called but I'm telling you, this just isn't enough. Besides, if that was a gun it's all over. All he has to do is claim you coerced him. I never should have used a damn amateur. I never should have let you do this."

"Sure, I pulled a gun on him and when he still wouldn't confess I shot myself in the leg to convince him I was serious. Besides, you've got him on the murder of VanDyk."

"We don't know that VanDyk is dead."

Just then Lyman uttered a low groan. "Oh, God." Kneeling in the sopping dirt, he dropped what he was holding and dabbed desperately at his filthy shirtfront to wipe his fingers. When Fresh stepped closer he saw what Lyman had dropped was a pair of severed hands. The nails were a bloodless neon-white, the skin was turning a bruised-blue-green and black, and the fingers curled into half-made fists. It was shock and the putrid smell that made Lyman retch uncontrolled vomit down the front of his shirt.

"There's a shovel somewhere around here. You can try the garage, that's where I'd look. I'd be willing to bet that it's got Lyman's fingerprints on the handle and Van-Dyk's blood on the blade." He paused for a moment. "You also probably have a corpse somewhere that needs a pair of those," Quitman said, pointing to the severed hands. "That enough?" he asked.

Against the canopy of the cold, damp, low night sky he could see the pulsing of the police lights, still miles below at the mouth of the canyon road.

"Stand up," Fresh hollered to Lyman. It took all his effort but he managed to drag the man to his feet. He handcuffed him and shoved him into the back of the police car.

"So what's this about two million dollars and a coin?" he asked Quitman as he used a corner of his handkerchief to clear splattered mud away from his eye.

Quitman put the coin in Fresh's hand and began, "I don't know where the two million might be but if it can be found you'll find it.

"As far as the coin's concerned, I don't know much but here's what I do know. Helen Costello was married to a James Meyers who worked for the mint. He kept that silver dollar even though they were supposed to be melted down, all of them, when the issue was cancelled." He responded to a questioning look from Fresh with a shrug and "Don't ask me, I don't know. The president, the congress, somebody cancelled it, and he had that one and he kept it. Because it's so rare, it's immensely valuable. I got it from Helen's. I just picked it up because that's the year I was born! Imagine that?

"As near as I can tell Hackett suspected I had it because I stopped in his shop one day to ask about coins from 1964. I mentioned the 64 D in an offhanded way and I think that's where it all started. They went after Marty because they thought it was me they were getting, and to get Hackett out of the deal. They went after Helen still trying to find a route to the coin."

"How does Maria fit in?" Fresh asked.

"As a friend, that's the only way Maria fits in. I sold her a car, we became friends. Let it go at that, will you? The equation is Helen, Marty, and me on one side and Hackett, Lyman, and VanDyk on the other. It's not very complex, really. After Marty and Helen they had no place else to go so they went back and undid the Hackett doublecross to get him back in. It was the only lead they had left. I think they finally went after me because they couldn't think of what else to do. With Hackett dead they were at another dead-end.

"Then," Quitman continued, "Lyman killed Van-Dyk."

"That part doesn't make any sense."

"VanDyk was the only connection left that tied Lyman to the first two murders."

"Why cut off his hands? Why bury them here?"

"Simple. One, to hamper identification, and, two, he didn't feel any hint of suspicion. He didn't think anyone was after him. Why would they be?"

"Why was he so horrified by finding the hands?"

"He wasn't horrified by finding them, he wasn't horrified at all. He was trapped and defeated, that's what you were seeing. Don't you have any imagination?"

Fresh's eyes scanned Quitman's face. He licked his lips, tucked at his rumpled shirt, cinched his pants up to his waist. "Is that all you have to say?"

"You're looking at me like you think I killed VanDyk but I didn't. If I did . . . if what I wanted was revenge I could've killed Lyman, too, couldn't I? But what did I do? I called you. I asked the law for help. Is that going to turn out to be my shortcoming, my downfall? I had the coin and a good hunch that a lot of money was lurking somewhere within Hackett's territorial range. Search his shop or apartment or safe deposit box and you'll come up with the cash. You'll be a hero. Why did I call you? Can't you just take this in your hands and make the pieces fit?

"You're looking for answers, so am I," Quitman continued. "What did Marty or Helen do to deserve any of this? Why are they dead a way long time before they should be, before it's natural? Can you tell me that by any chance? I loved her, Fresh. But I'm angry at everybody, including her, because she's dead. But even that, even my anger won't do me or anybody any good. Death changes everything. I know it's stupid to say that, it's so trite, but now that she's dead all the rules are different. There are no options open to me, none that I can live with, but forgiveness. I have to at least be able to forgive myself for my selfishness, and forgive her for dying right when I didn't want her to. At least that. And I'll never be able to do even that, even something as simple as that, unless some kind of justice takes place here. Justice, Fresh, not procedural correctness, not Miranda, not protocols written by insurance actuaries: *Justice*. The 'terrible swift sword' thing. Can't you understand that?''

A long silence passed between them. Fresh looked down at the coin resting in his palm. He read the large word to himself that the engraver had inscribed across the back of this coin that was to be the reissue of the true silver dollar: PEACE.

"I'll need this coin for evidence," he began. "You can have it back when this is over. I'll write you a receipt."

Quitman looked beyond Fresh. Two police cars pulled up and splayed themselves along the edge of the grass where a curb would have been. The whining sirens ground to silence, leaving the flashing lights to dance unaccompanied, reflecting across the low overhead mist.

A uniformed sergeant and one other officer jogged over to Fresh. Without the question being asked Fresh answered, "Secure the house, perimeter first, then interior."

"Yes, Sir," the sergeant answered. With her hand on the butt of the automatic pistol riding high on her hip, she indicated Quitman with her eyes and said, "This individual, Sir, a Friendly?"

Fresh thought a moment. He opened his jacket to display to the sergeant that he was still armed and that the small snap-on button they used as a code to indicate that the gun was in fact loaded and that he was in control of the situation and not under any duress or undue influence, was in place as it should be. "Yes, Sergeant, a Friendly."

The sergeant held her noncommittal gaze on Quitman for a moment longer. The result of her assessment never became apparent. She simply turned and jogged back toward the other waiting officers.

"You were talking about the receipt?" Quitman said. "You met Betty Martinez, Marty's widow, and his little girl, Gloria?"

"Yeah, I was, and I do remember them. I interviewed them about Marty's death. Why?" Fresh asked.

"Give it to her. Make the receipt out to the child, Gloria, will you? See that the kid gets it?"

"Didn't it belong to the woman, to Helen Costello?"

"Why bring that up?"

"If it was hers her relatives have a claim."

"She didn't have any relatives. Her late husband had a sister but I'm not even sure if she'd still be considered her sister-in-law since her husband's dead. Besides, who did you notify as next of kin?"

"No one," Fresh replied.

"There you go. That makes it pretty simple, doesn't it? Look at this, too. You know who was at the funeral besides me? Same answer. No one. Don't let this get bogged down in bureaucratic bullshit, Fresh. They'll never look for anybody. They'll drop it in a vault somewhere till the statute of limitations runs out then they'll sell it and use the money to buy cars for some fucking politician or to build one crummy fucking inch of free-way somewhere. What's *just* about that?"

Fresh pulled his receipt book from the glove compartment of his car. "Gloria? Any middle name, do you know?" he said, writing.

"Must have, I suppose, but I don't know. Ask her mother," Quitman said, as he started up the drive toward his car.

"What about you, your leg?"

"I'll be alright."

"I've got an ambulance coming."

Quitman lied, "I've got a first aid kit in the car. Use the ambulance for the fat man." He stopped and turned back, looked at Fresh and smiled. He wasn't sure from that distance if there wasn't a slight smile on Fresh's face as well, as he turned and walked away from him.

Nineteen

Quitman pulled his car out of the bushes, turned it around and pointed it down the hill. His headlight beams hung in the foggy air like cardboard cutouts of beams of light, imitations of the real thing. That was the way he was beginning to feel about the whole experience, as if it was an imitation of an experience rather than the experience itself. Was that another cardboard cutout he sensed? This time of an evergreen tree infused with the scent of pine and tucked away in the car somewhere as an air freshener, or was it the real aroma of the towering thicket of fir that surrounded him?

When he had nearly reached the bottom of Apache Canyon he realized that Skyline Road and Xerxes were more than five miles behind him. They were both farther away and closer than any simple measure of distance could ever be able to indicate. They were in a box in the back of his brain with other facts and feelings that were too painful to assimilate, at least for the present. At least for right now.

The road at the mouth of the canyon ran north and south and, if you had cared to ask, he could not have told you which direction he would choose.